WHERE CARRION GODS DANCE

WHERE CARRION GODS DANCE

By

Brad C. Hodson

Washington Park Press
Los Angeles CA

Where Carrion Gods Dance
Copyright © 2019 Brad Hodson

ISBN-13: 9780578585000
ISBN-10: 0578585006

First Edition

"Haunted" © 2014, originally published at
www.halloweenforevermore.com
"The Other Patrick" © 2012, originally published in *Horror For Good*
"Il Donnaiolo" © 2010, originally published in *Werewolves and Shapeshifters: Encounters with the Beasts Within*
"The Perfect Jackson" © 2008, originally published in *Not One of Us: Home and Away*
"Breathe" © 2012, originally published in *Slices of Flesh*
"In the Halls and on the Stairs" © 2013, originally published in *Nightscapes Vol 1*
"The Scottish Play" © 2014, originally published in *Hell Comes to Hollywood II*
"Almost" © 2014, originally published in *Dark Fuse: Horror d'oeuvres*
"His Only Company, the Walls" © 2010, originally published in *Voices*
"Picked Last" © 2007, originally published in *Midnight Lullabies*
"Chasing the Reaper" © 2019, original to this collection
"Tabula Rasa" © 2017, originally published in *Unspeakable Horror 2*
"Hester Cohen" © 2019, original to this collection
"Biology" © 2013, originally published in *I Will Rise Limited Edition*
"Where Carrion Gods Dance" © 2007, originally published in *Dred*
"The Thousandth Hell" © 2013, originally published in After Death
"The Lord of Misrule" © 2019, original to this collection

In Memory of James O'Neill

So, we'll go no more a roving
So late into the night,
Though the heart be still as loving,
And the moon be still as bright.

For the sword outwears its sheath,
And the soul wears out the breast,
And the heart must pause to breathe,
And love itself have rest.

Though the night was made for loving,
And the day returns too soon,
Yet we'll go no more a roving
By the light of the moon.

—*Lord Byron*

TABLE OF CONTENTS

INTRODUCTION

Dumpster Stories

On Halloween night in 1997, I thought I'd killed someone.

It was the autumn following high school graduation and I had been hired as a bouncer at Moose's Music Hall. Moose's opened earlier that year and had already made a name for itself on the Strip as a popular, albeit rough, drinking hole. It was an odd place, the downstairs your classic sports bar with wooden decor and video games, a few pool tables in the back. Upstairs, behind metal doors painted red, sat a stage and massive dance floor, another bar opening onto a patio they sometimes filled with foam for bikini dance parties.

At the time, I lived in a house affectionately dubbed by its occupants "The House of Ill Repute." My roommates included a roadie for GWAR, a Chinese bodybuilder with an almost supernatural ability to spot fake IDs, a male dancer studying to be a lawyer, and the trumpet player for a local ska band. They all had worked at Moose's in various capacities and so it was only natural, I suppose, that I'd end up there, too.

My only reference point for bouncing at the time had been the movie *Roadhouse*. I took Swayze's mantras to heart:

Be nice until it's time not to be nice. Pain don't hurt. Take it outside.

I was maybe a buck sixty-five at the time and not much of an imposing presence, so I got stationed in the back room downstairs. It was quiet for the most part and, on the rare occasion I needed to escort someone out, I prided myself on the fact I could do it without any violence. You'd be surprised how well even the drunkest redneck will react to, "I'm sorry, man, I'm just doing my job."

Then this Halloween night, the Misfits are playing, the entire club decked out in orange and black streamers. Cardboard cutouts of ghosts in chains and witches on brooms and hissing black cats had been hung everywhere. One of the other bouncers, a massive horse of a man with squinty eyes and a big buck tooth smile, hauled this kid into the back room. The bouncer was dressed in a gray and blue Batman suit, his gut hanging over the yellow belt. The kid wore white face-paint, black circling his eyes and mouth. He couldn't have been older than I was, which means he was at least three years under the legal drinking age in Tennessee.

Three sheets to the wind, he slurred his words and stared at nothing as he begged and pleaded not to be thrown out.

"Zis my fave-rit band, man. Doan may me leave."

Batman handed him off and went back to his position up by the stage.

I had never received the memo about costumes and so hadn't dressed up. Halloween has always been my favorite holiday and I was more than a little bummed out to be the only one that night wearing my blue "Security" T-shirt. I escorted the kid out the back door and down the black steel stairs leading into the alley below. The "I'm just doing my job" schtick seemed to be working as he pleaded and apologized.

Once in the alley and off the property, I wished him a good night and headed back up the stairs.

"Fuck you, man," he yelled. "Asshole! Pussy!"

This was such a complete 180-degree-turn in his attitude that I could only stop and stare down at him.

"I bet you ain't even a real bouncer. You're too small. What a stupid ass costume. You stupid ass!"

He flipped me the bird and then, examining his finger in the air as though he'd made a mistake, raised his other hand and extended that middle-finger, too. He nodded twice, a smile on his face like he'd been trying to figure out flipping someone off for some time now and it had finally clicked.

"Go on, pal," I said, taking a step back down toward him. "You're drunk. Get out of here."

He spewed a series of "fucks" and "shits" and "cock-suckers" and every homophobic slur you could imagine.

Then he picked a rock up off the ground and chucked it at me.

Let's just say he never would have made it in the majors. The rock bounced from the wall of the club to fall back to the ground.

Not wanting to see if his aim improved on subsequent throws, I descended into the alley. He took a step away, his rational mind surely telling him to leave.

His lizard brain must have taken over instead because he swung at me.

I rushed in, crowding him, the punch sailing past my head, and grabbed his shoulders, spinning him around quickly until he was in a choke hold. I kicked his feet out from under him, dragged him backward, and cinched it.

I'd never choked anyone out before so, when he went still in my arms and I dropped him, I was surprised to see how limp he'd gone. He crumpled to the alley floor, head on his shoulder, back bent, knees splayed. It was like dropping a rag doll.

"Hey," I said. "Hey, man. You okay?"

No answer.

I gave him a couple of light slaps on the face, but he didn't so much as open his eyes.

Suddenly, old news stories I'd seen about suspects dying from chokeholds administered by the police ran through my head. Did this guy have one of the conditions that could make a choke lethal? What were those conditions, even? Were they common? Why hadn't they briefed me on any of this when they hired me?

Had I just killed someone?

I looked around. No one else was in the alley. No windows looked down on us. The only sound was the muffled guitar chords leaking from the walls of Moose's.

"C'mon, man," I said, a whiny desperation in my voice as I tried to stand the guy back on his feet.

His dead weight slipped right out of my arms.

Oh, shit.

I killed this guy.

Ohshitohshitohshit.

Cars sometimes took that alley as a shortcut and the next thought I had was that I should get him out of the way. If a car came through and plowed into him...?

Well, I didn't want to think about that.

So, I hefted him onto my shoulders in a fireman's carry and walked to a dumpster.

Standing there in the cool autumn breeze, flies buzzing around the sour smell of old beer, an idea came to me. It wasn't an idea I'm proud of. I was, after all, an eighteen-year-old kid panicking with what I thought was a corpse over my shoulders. But the thought was this:

Put him in the dumpster. Just drop him in, go back inside, and pretend nothing happened. When they find him, say you escorted him out the back door and never saw him again. You have no idea what happened or how he ended up dead in a pile of trash.

One of the great shames of my life is how long I stood there actually considering this.

Finally, the guy groaned on my back.

"You're alive!" I yelled. "Hallelujah, you're alive!"

I shrugged him down and placed him on his feet.

When I let go, he fell over with a thud.

"Oh," I said. "Sorry."

He groaned, eyes still closed, and placed his fingers on his temples in the universal *I have a headache* sign.

I trotted back over to the stairs, climbed halfway up, and sat there for what felt an eternity. Finally, he fought to his feet, looked around confused, and stumbled from the alley.

Thank the gods for that. As thematically appropriate as it would have been to murder someone and dump their corpse on Halloween, I cannot overstate how relieved I was it had never happened.

But I was stained now, you see. I knew all too well how easy it would be to kill someone and cover it up. Not even out of anger or jealousy or greed. I'd simply defended myself and then panicked after the fact.

It's a funny story, one I usually tell to get a few laughs over drinks. I don't typically dwell on the coldness of my self-preservation instincts when doing so. Where's the fun in that?

It's still there, though. Lurking. Waiting to take over again. I know that now. There's a dark core to all of us. I don't mean that in any kind of Puritanical righteousness, nor in pessimism about the human race. I believe most people are good people struggling to get by. To agree with a certain lawyer from Illinois, I believe in the better angels of our nature.

But that doesn't mean the animal inside of us has disappeared. It waits, ready to give way to fear or anger or any number of vices. What makes someone a good person isn't the absence of this dark side but, rather, one's willingness to battle it.

And, sometimes, people lose that battle.

Those are the stories that interest me.

The tales in this book cross several themes, many of which I wasn't even aware of until years after I'd written them. Stories are funny like that. They're born from the sum of who you are at the moment you jot them down. This means they draw from even your most hidden places, those strange and shadowy parts you haven't found until you've gained some distance from them. There's horror in them thar hills and it comes scurrying down when you least expect it.

And why shouldn't it? The best stories work on the subconscious. Horror stories in particular (the genre for most—though not all—of what you'll find here) lean toward a kind of nightmare logic that falls apart upon scrutiny. Rationality, to paraphrase the man from Maine, is antithetical to the poetry of fear.

Thus, you'll find here stories of unimaginable loss and the cruelty of childhood. You'll find tales of sexual obsession and the lengths we go to when lying to ourselves. Several stories are about navigating that false brand of masculinity that tells men they're not allowed to hurt, that tells them power comes only from causing pain to others, that makes them fail at being husbands and fathers and friends.

You'll find, too, characters who needed help and were denied it by those closest to them, their mental illness left untreated when the signs were so obvious, and the gruesome minefield that is that nebulous region between childhood and adulthood.

You'll also find ghosts and revenants, creepy houses and dark rituals, werewolves and vampires and bears, oh my! Hopefully you'll laugh some and be saddened a bit and maybe, if I did my job well, sleep with the lights on for a night or two.

But the best I can hope for is that you come away with a little empathy for those who haven't been able to fight their battles as well as you have.

Of course, that's assuming you've won all your battles. Surely you have your own Halloween dumpster story, don't you?

Maybe your story's even worse.

Maybe your drunken college kid never woke up.

Maybe you tossed him into that dumpster. Maybe you lied to the police and to the kid's family after his body was found. Maybe he came to visit you one dark night, scratching on your window and begging to be let in.

That, or something worse, could be *your* dumpster story.

If you have one.

I hope you have one. Because if you don't...

Well. Maybe your story just hasn't happened.

Yet.

Brad C. Hodson
Los Angeles, CA
July 2019

HAUNTED

People swore the house was haunted. The stories had circulated since my grandfather was young.

"I never believed it," he said one October night as we sat on the back porch, a beer sweating in his hand. This was the year he passed and those hands that had smacked my bottom when I misbehaved now trembled, the skin paper thin and spotted. "I been all over and every place I ever seen had a house filled with haints. You boys'd do better staying here and talking with your Grandpa."

I wanted nothing more. My grandfather was a superhero to me, a man who'd been everywhere and seen everything. Since Grandma died, he loved to sit on the porch and tell us stories. Most of the crazier ones were lies, I'm sure of it, but I loved listening all the same.

James made a face behind Grandpa's chair and I knew we were going. My brother had always been adventurous and nothing short of Mark Twain's ghost materializing on the porch would have kept him from exploring a haunted house at Halloween. I was at the age that wherever my brother went, I followed. We don't talk much since he moved to New York, but in those days, I was glued to James.

After he assembled his ghost hunting kit (little more than a flashlight, a Bible, and a pack of cigarettes), we hopped from the porch and sprinted through the shadows in the yard.

I glanced over my shoulder before following James down the street. Grandpa leaned against a post, one hand held high.

I waved back.

Mom and Dad would have lost it if they knew we left, but Grandpa understood what it was like to be a boy. Maybe life is circular that way, clear images of the beginning not returning until the end. Whatever the reason, we were confident he'd keep our secret.

The house turned out to be more hype than reality. If ghosts did haunt the halls, they had taken the night off. We crawled in through a broken window in the back, crunching through leaves blanketing the floor. The wood smelled of dust and mold and I followed James into a room upstairs where we waited for something to materialize.

"You know they say most people don't see the ghost here," James said after we'd sat a while with nothing happening. "But that's worse."

"What do you mean?"

"It don't like people trespassing here none. If you see it, that means it didn't know you were here."

"What's it mean if you don't see it?"

He grinned, the red-tipped nub of his cigarette between his teeth. "That means it saw you."

I squirmed, suddenly uncomfortable. "So?"

"So, it's a spiteful thing. Who knows what it might do?"

"How did he die?" I asked.

"She," my brother said. "I think. There's a bunch of stories about this place. None of them really seem to know what happened here. I heard she hung herself. Tommy Peters done said she got murdered by a hobo. Either way, she ain't never found peace."

"What's a hobo?"

"You know," he said. "A hobo." As if that explained anything.

The hall stretching out before us was dark without even a trickle of moonlight to spoil the black. I stared into it and wondered if that's what awaited us all when our time was up. Would the stories of us be all that remained?

As the night wore on, my brother inducted me into the secrets of smoking and showed me my first Playboy. He'd stolen it from Dad's closet just that morning. The feeling that this was a turning point, that I entered a new phase of boyhood, held me the entire night.

We made our way home a few hours later, bored and tired of fighting off the roaches and spiders that filled the house. When we reached the yard, laughing and sweating despite the cold wind, James grabbed my shoulder.

"Wait here," he said, eyes wide.

My brother ran to where our grandfather's twisted body wheezed on the porch. His back to us and knees curled to his chest, he trembled.

Ignoring my brother's command, I darted across the yard.

"Stay with him," James said and stood. "I'm gonna call an ambulance." He rushed inside.

I took my grandfather's hand and whispered to him, tears streaking my face. His beer was overturned on the top step, dark liquid dripping down into the yard. He stared at nothing and struggled for breath.

They say he'd had a stroke while we were gone. If he had received immediate assistance he may have recovered. Instead, left there alone, he lost the use of his right side. A few months later, a second stroke came and stole him away.

My brother had been right. Whatever was in that house was a spiteful thing indeed.

THE OTHER PATRICK

He wanted to leave the cemetery but his wife ignored him, Anna too intent on finding the graves of old Hollywood stars. They'd only been in Los Angeles for a month, David's public relations firm deciding that now would be the perfect time to diversify and dabble in show business. He hated Hollywood, hated the celebrity culture, and especially hated trudging through cemeteries.

Anna loved every minute of it. "Modern Hollywood is fine," she'd said as they entered the cemetery, "but 'The Golden Age' was so glamorous and exciting."

Even though she knew David would hate it, she insisted on visiting the final resting places of Rudolph Valentino and Faye Wray. He'd made the mistake of being critical of Douglas Fairbanks Junior's massive Roman tomb, complete with a very Caesar-like bust of himself and a reflecting pool, and thought he'd never hear the end of it.

"He was a legend," Anna had said.

"He was a narcissist. He didn't do anything to change the world for better or worse."

"He entertained people. Sometimes that's all we need."

This was what he got for marrying someone with her head in the clouds. He saw her interest in acting as a hobby. Every time they argued about ridiculous things like this, they both knew it was just a front for the real tension: she didn't feel her husband respected her.

He did, though. He respected her. He just didn't see why something as self-serving as acting was considered a lofty goal. Not that he had some higher purpose he served, but at least he didn't pretend to, either.

They rounded a corner in the path and Anna ran down the hill. "David. Come look at this."

He walked toward her expecting to find a golden statue of Larry, Moe, and Curly in togas. When he saw what had captivated his wife, the joke he was about to make died on his lips.

A long wall of hedges ran along the boundary of the cemetery. Small tombstones pressed against their length and long, brown vines scrambled up them. What chilled David and obviously fascinated his wife, who snapped picture after picture on her phone, were the toys. Thousands of them tangled in the vines as offerings to the graves beneath. The empty glass eyes of molded dolls peeked out from behind green leaves while dirty action figures scaled a wall they would never reach the top of. From a distance, the faded plastic had almost looked like a flower arrangement.

He knelt in front of one. The boy had only been six when he died. The toys surrounding the grave were old and discolored. A small porcelain doll, a wooden train, and two GI Joes. Someone had burned the soldiers' faces off.

Other graves were similarly decorated. Faded pink dollhouses and fire trucks rusted brown, soggy stuffed animals and plastic tea sets stained the color of soot. Superheroes fought with ivy that threatened to swallow them and plastic circus animals sunk into the dirt at their feet. The entire memorial ran the length of a small city block.

"Morbid," he said.

"I think it's beautiful." Anna snapped away with her cell phone.

The sun reflected from a tear rolling down her cheek and David turned away.

"I think one of the Ramones is buried over here." He walked away from the wall. He didn't want her to bring it up, was afraid of the topic since she mentioned visiting the cemetery. He didn't turn around to see if she was following. He knew she would wait long enough to compose herself and then catch up with him.

"Oh my God," she said, and his heart sank. "David. Oh my God, look at this."

He returned to the wall. She was on one knee, face streaked with tears and breathing heavy.

He placed a hand on her shoulder. "Anna..." he started.

"David, the name..."

He stared at the engraving. The letters didn't make sense. He shook his head and looked again, unable to process what was carved into the stone. He could see the letters, but no syllables formed.

Finally, it came to him: *Patrick Neil Cunningham, Dec 1st, 2012– July 18th, 2016.*

"Jesus."

"I know." She gripped his hand and squeezed it, squeezed it so hard his fingers lost all sensation. "What does it mean?"

"Nothing. Nothing at all. It's just a bizarre coincidence." It had to be a coincidence. It was too strange.

"But the name—"

"Cunningham's a pretty common name," he said.

"But all three names?"

"It happens. I went to high school with another David Neil Cunningham. I even had a college professor named Neil David Cunningham."

"Yeah." She didn't seem convinced. She sniffed and rubbed her eyes with the back of her free hand. "Yeah, you're right. The months were the same and that got me."

"But still off by a year and some change on both ends."

They sat in silence a moment, staring at the grave. He surveyed the toys strung around it. A small stuffed dog with a plastic tear in his eye and his arm in a sling. The sling said "Boo-Boo." Above that and to the right was a collection of firemen, soldiers, and police officers that looked like they were part of a Lego set. A big, yellow Tonka dump truck sat on a rock underneath them.

He nearly gasped when he saw the doll.

It was brown, sewn together from a burlap sack, black buttons for eyes and a mouth of dark thread. It wore faded blue overalls cut from an old pair of jeans.

He stood and grabbed Anna's shoulder, hoping she hadn't seen it. "Let's go check out the graves over here."

"Huh? Oh, sure. Yeah." She stood and dusted off her knees. Her hand wrapped around his again, not quite so tight this time, and they walked away.

Thank God she didn't see it.

"I'm sorry I was snippy with you earlier," she said.

"I'm sorry I'm such an asshole."

"It's okay. I knew you were an asshole when I married you." She smiled. "It's part of your charm."

He laughed, glad her mood had improved.

On the drive home they talked about work, Anna's latest audition, and traffic. Anything but Patrick. It was pained and awkward, both aware that his name was on the tips of their tongues. He might as well be in the car, David thought. But Anna's laughter, even if forced, meant that she had dealt with it.

At home, Anna drew a hot bath for herself and David returned a call to an old client back in D.C. They ordered Chinese for dinner, watched a movie, and made love. It was slow and sweet, but not passionate. It was more comforting than anything, like a warm fire on a cold day.

When he was sure she was asleep, he crept into the living room and sifted through the boxes in the closet. When he found the one labeled "Patrick," he pulled it down and took it into the bathroom in case Anna woke up.

He shut the door behind him, careful not to make too much noise. The faucet dripped and he made a mental note to call the landlord for the third time about repairing it. Lowering himself onto the toilet seat, he rested the box on his lap.

He shivered when he opened it, unsure if it was because

of the cold plastic seat pressing against his thighs or the sight of Patrick's clothes folded so neatly inside. He had tried to donate them to Goodwill before they moved but couldn't bring himself to do it. He'd even gone so far as packing them in a garbage bag and leaving them on the porch but had snatched the bag back inside at the last moment.

Grabbing the shirt on top, he removed it tenderly, as though it might crumble to dust. It unfolded in his hands. Big Bird's bright blue eyes stared at him. Patrick loved Big Bird.

David pulled the shirt to his face, felt the soft cotton against his cheek. He closed his eyes and inhaled. The shirt smelled like grass and orange juice. It smelled like Patrick.

Tears welled up in his eyes. There in the bathroom, alone and shielded from the world, he let himself cry.

When he was done, he placed the shirt on the floor with the same care as when he'd taken it out of the box. He turned back and pulled out the rest of Patrick's clothes.

He removed a blanket and this time he did gasp.

There was the doll.

It was almost identical to the one at the cemetery. The only difference was the denim dress it wore, a remnant from before Patrick was born. After his birth, David's mother corrected her mistake by making a boy version. That was the doll Patrick was buried with. Looking at its sister, David was positive it was the twin of the one in the cemetery.

It's a coincidence, he reminded himself. The one at the graveyard was probably made by that poor kid's grandmother, too. It must have been be a popular thing for women from that generation.

He studied the doll for a few moments, traced his fingers along the stitching that held its cotton ball stuffing in place. Then he wiped his eyes, sealed it back in its box, and returned it to the closet.

He didn't sleep well that night. The dark often brought

loneliness and the loneliness brought dreams of his son. Patrick in his playpen with the doll. Patrick's fourth birthday party at the park. Patrick throwing his ball into the neighbor's yard. Their dog barking. Patrick wandering over and the dog breaking free of its leash and Anna screaming and—

The alarm clock's buzzing yanked him from the dream. He rolled over, hit snooze, and closed his eyes. He needed another half an hour. But when his eyes shut again, Patrick was there. The boy's blond hair fell into his eyes as he smiled. He held the doll to his chest.

David rolled out of bed and showered.

Anna climbed into the shower with him. "Morning," she said.

"Morning." He lathered up his hair.

"Did you call the landlord about that faucet?"

He shook his head. "Can you do it?"

"Sure." She yawned. "How did you sleep?" She maneuvered past him for the shampoo.

"Not very well."

"Bad dreams?"

"Yeah."

"Me too."

That was the closest they came to discussing their son.

His day ground on between paperwork and mind-numbing conference calls. On his lunch break he found himself driving past the cemetery. He thought about the doll, the name on the grave. It was all just a coincidence. Maybe the name was spelled differently, or the doll wasn't quite constructed the same.

Screw it.

He parked at a Subway down the street, bought himself a sandwich, and walked to the cemetery.

As he approached the wall, the same chill shot through him as the first time he saw Patrick's grave.

No, he thought, the *other* Patrick.

He crouched until he was face to face with the doll. It

had the same type of construction, the same stitching, and the same eyes and mouth as the one in his closet.

The coincidence was too strange. He reached for it, brushed its burlap cheek. His fingers wrapped around it and tugged. A part of his mind screamed, *What the hell do you think you're doing?* but his hand worked for itself and pulled the doll away.

He was going to get caught. Someone would bust him. Could they charge him with grave robbing for this? He didn't know.

He tucked the doll in his jacket and hurried back to work.

The rest of the day, the doll stayed in his jacket pocket. Every now and then, he would reach his fingers in to feel the coarse burlap or trace the line of its mouth. He fought the urge to pull it out and stare at it. He didn't want to explain to everyone in his office why he was playing with a doll.

A doll stolen from a child's grave.

Why did he do that?

Every time he touched it, he imagined his son's doll tucked between his arm and chest in his coffin. His son's fingers curled around its body, hugging it tight against the navy-blue suit he was buried in, the holes in his son's flesh sewn together and painted over with make-up.

When he arrived home, he went to the closet and hung his jacket up. Anna walked in as he closed the door.

She grinned. "Putting up your own things, huh?"

"Yeah."

"About time," she joked.

"Don't start with that," he said. He regretted it as he watched her smile fade. He didn't know why he snapped at her, especially when she had been in such a good mood.

She nodded, her face stone, and went into the kitchen.

David sighed and sat on the couch. He felt the faint stirrings of a headache coming. Closing his eyes, he massaged his temples and wondered why he wasn't a better husband.

Anna cooked spaghetti and they went for a long walk. They didn't speak much. David was too focused on the doll. When she went to bed, he took it from his jacket and collapsed onto the couch. He held it above him and examined it, running his fingers along every curve.

He should return it. What if the other Patrick's parents came by and noticed it missing? How would they feel?

Tomorrow. He'd take it back on his lunch break.

He fell asleep on the couch with the doll in his arms and wasn't out long when something jolted him awake. Bolting upright, the doll fell from his lap into the floor.

"Anna, I..."

She wasn't there. The door to the bedroom was still closed.

His hand went to his cheek. What was it that woke him? He thought he had felt Anna's hand on his face.

He must have been dreaming. He leaned over and reached for the doll.

It wasn't there.

It had fallen beside the couch. He was sure of it. He rolled onto the floor and crawled around patting under the furniture. A sick feeling started to form in the pit of his stomach. What if he couldn't find the doll?

What if Anna found it instead?

He sat on his knees and ran a hand through his hair.

The doll was on the couch, facing him.

He blinked. Shook his head. He must have grabbed it when it fell and, half asleep, put it back on the couch without realizing it. It was a wonder he didn't carry it to bed with him.

He picked it up and returned it to his jacket, then shut the closet door and leaned his forehead against it. Eyes closed, he pressed his head harder against the door, feeling the grain of the wood against his skin. He pressed even harder, until little white lights sparked behind his lids, and imagined he pushed against the lid of a coffin.

After brushing his teeth, he stared at himself in the

mirror. Why was this hitting him so hard now, three years later? He grieved when his son died, as any father would. But his thoughts were never so macabre.

Maybe he'd been hiding his feelings for too long. Maybe avoiding them had only let the pressure build and now it went off like a tea kettle.

Or maybe it was the doll. Why did he take that thing anyway? He vowed again to return it tomorrow.

He crept into the bedroom, careful not to disturb his wife. She lay on her side with her back to him, the covers kicked off and tangled around her feet. Her hair spilled over her pillow and onto his half of the bed. He kicked off his clothes and slid in next to her, carefully gathering her hair and placing it over her shoulder. The bed swallowed him as he leaned onto his pillow.

He was almost asleep again when the door creaked. He must not have closed it all the way.

There was a faint shuffling, the sound of feet moving through carpet.

Heart racing, throat constricting, he tried to open his eyes, but his lids refused.

The shuffling grew closer. David tried to say Anna's name, but could barely breathe.

"Shhhh..."

He forced his eyes open at the sound. A small figure stood beside his bed.

Tears formed in David's eyes. "Patrick?"

"Yes."

He wiped his face and leaned forward. The figure was little more than shadow but the right size. The boy's brown hair hung down into his face, helping to hide his features.

His *brown* hair.

"You're not my son."

It placed a dry, withered finger to David's lips. The finger tasted like mold.

"I never said I was," the boy whispered. His voice was high pitched and playful. It was also hollow, like a recording played through blown speakers.

"You're the other Patrick." David sat up. His heartbeat slowed as he realized he must be dreaming.

The boy nodded.

David assumed he had come for the doll. "I was going to bring it back to you," he said.

Little fingers curled around his hand and tugged. David stood and followed the boy through the door.

They were in the cemetery. It was still night, the only light a sliver of moon that hung above their heads. David turned and looked behind him. They had stepped from a large, granite mausoleum. The iron door was open, and he could see his bedroom through it. Anna tossed and turned on their bed.

The fingers tugged again, and David followed.

As they neared the wall of hedges, he saw movement. Shadows flickered around the graves. He squinted, trying to puzzle out the scene.

They were playing.

Children gathered around their tombstones, pushing cars around in the dirt. Two boys placed army men on a small hill while a group of girls held a tea party around a rotting doll house.

As David approached, they stopped. Countless pairs of dead eyes fell on him.

"You took my doll," the other Patrick said.

Out here in the cemetery, under the moonlight, he could see the boy's pale skin and black eyes. Tiny threads of stitching hung from his eyelids and lips. A red T-shirt sat loose underneath a pair of overalls. He reminded David of the doll.

"I'm sorry."

"It's okay. I don't mind sharing. We all share our toys here."

The others turned back to their toys and continued playing.

"I just thought," the boy continued, "you might want to play with us."

"What?"

"You and the lady seem sad. Why?"

"My son..." David choked on the words.

"He has a doll like mine, huh? Was his name Patrick, too?"

David nodded.

"It's good to have toys when you come here," the other Patrick said. "Will you stay?"

A sinking feeling formed in David's stomach and he started to sweat. He shook his head.

The boy smiled. "It's okay. We're not lonely here. I just thought you might be. Do you want to play a while?"

"Okay."

One of the girls brought over a soggy and faded "Chutes and Ladders" game. "Hi. I'm Alessa."

She opened the box and pulled the board out. Her long hair hung down over a faded blue dress. David guessed her hair had once been blond but had faded to the color of grub worms.

"This is David," the other Patrick said.

"It's nice to meet you. We don't get a lot of grown-ups playing with us anymore. What piece do you want?"

David pointed to one of the pieces at random. Alessa handed it to him and frowned.

"It's a lot yuckier than it used to be," she said, embarrassed.

"My toys have gotten pretty yucky, too," Patrick said.

"It's okay," David said. "I don't mind."

They played the game for hours, until the rising sun shot streaks of purple through the sky.

"I should take you back," Patrick said.

Alessa smiled and gathered the game pieces up. "It was nice playing with you, David. You're a sweet man." She took her box and rushed back over to the wall of graves.

Patrick's tiny fingers wrapped around David's and tugged him back toward the mausoleum. "Will you play with us again tomorrow?"

"Sure. Yeah, I will." David smiled and stepped through the door.

He showered and left before Anna woke, leaving a note that he had an early meeting. Hopefully she wouldn't call and discover he he'd cancelled his meetings and called in sick.

He drove to the cemetery and parked out front. He waited an hour for the gates to open and then rushed to the wall. His eyes scanned up and down, running over each of the rotting toys.

There it was. The "Chutes and Ladders" game wedged deep into the growth above a small grave. He ripped the vines and weeds away and fell to his knees when he saw the name.

Alessa Orinkov.

It was real. It happened. He had spent the night playing here with these children. He shook his head in disbelief. Blinked. Read the name again.

He stood and stumbled over to Patrick's grave. He took the doll from his jacket and tied it back in place. Scanning up and down the wall again, he noted which toys were in the worst condition. Then he left.

"Thank you for the toys," Patrick said as the children pulled their presents from the vines.

Laughter echoed through the empty cemetery and filled David with warmth. It was like watching his son on Christmas morning. "I brought your doll back, too," David said.

"I know. But I want you to keep it." Patrick handed it back.

"You sure?"

Patrick smiled and tugged on David's hand. "I'm glad you come to see us so much. My Dad stopped coming. He only visited during the day, with the other grownups. But he doesn't even do that now."

"I'm sorry."

"It made him too sad."

David understood how that felt. He ruffled the boy's hair. "I'm sure he'll be back."

"At least I've got you to play with me now."

Alessa ran to David, hugging her brand new "Chutes and Ladders" to her chest. "Thank you. Oh, thank you-thank you-thank-you."

He played with all the children that night, showing each of them how to use their new toys. It made him feel good inside, like he was human again. Like he was a father again.

※ ※ ※

"Why have you been lying to me?" Anna was angry, angrier than David had seen her in a long while. But he knew she was hurt, too, and so he kept his voice calm.

"I didn't mean to lie to you."

"Why haven't you been to work in a week?"

"I haven't been sleeping well." He shuffled his feet and looked at the floor, unsure what to tell her.

"Then where have you been going in the morning when you leave here? Why have you withdrawn six hundred dollars from our checking account?" Her face was fire and little flecks of spittle flew from her mouth.

"You wouldn't understand."

"Is it another woman?" Her body shook as she asked it and David's insides hollowed from what he was putting her through.

"No. God no."

"Then what is it?"

"Patrick." He blurted it without thinking. It hung in the air between them and there was no turning back.

She sat on the bed next to him. They were both quiet.

Finally Anna touched a hand to his knee and asked, "What do you mean?"

"Can I show you something?"

She nodded. David went to the closet and brought back Patrick's box. Anna started to cry as he removed their son's clothes. Her hand went to them, and then recoiled as if she had burned herself. Finally, he revealed the doll.

He held it toward her. "Do you remember this?"

She nodded, refusing to touch it.

"Do you remember the one we buried him with?"

"Why are you doing this to me?"

He pulled the other Patrick's doll from his jacket. Her hands went to her mouth and she shook her head back and forth.

"I found this at the cemetery," he said.

"What?"

"It was at Patrick's grave. The other Patrick. The grave you and I saw that day."

"Why would you take it?"

"I don't know. I just wanted to... I don't know." He shook his head.

"Oh, David. You have to take it back."

"I tried. He told me to keep it."

"Who?"

He swallowed. "The other Patrick. The one at the cemetery."

She stood and paced over to the window. Staring out, she wiped her eyes and took a deep breath. "We need to see a counselor. You've never dealt with his death."

"And you have?"

"I don't know. But this isn't normal, David. It's not sane."

He could agree with that.

But it was real. He knew it was.

"I'm sorry I wasn't there for you like I should have been," he said. "After he died, I shouldn't have shut myself off from you. Shouldn't have poured myself into work instead of into us."

He waited for her to say something, but she continued to stare out the window.

"I'm sorry I never supported your acting," he went on. "It's not just a hobby. I know that now. It's a calling. Something you're drawn to do."

She nodded.

David went into the kitchen and poured them each a glass of water. He placed hers on the nightstand with two sleeping pills. He gulped down two himself and curled up on his side of the bed, the doll clutched to his chest.

Later, as he drifted off to sleep, he thought he felt her reach around him and take the doll.

When he heard Anna gasp, he opened his eyes and rolled over to find her sitting up, the doll in her hands. She trembled and whispered something. He put his hand on her knee, but she couldn't take her eyes from the figure that had entered the room.

"It's okay." David stood and took Patrick's hand. "Come with us," he said and reached for her.

She stared at his hand for a long while before taking it and crawling from the bed.

❊ ❊ ❊

When they were in the cemetery, Patrick ran to the children already playing with their new toys at the wall.

Anna was sobbing. "Oh my God, oh my God."

David held her. "Shhhh. It's okay. They just want to play." He led his wife to the wall. "This is what I've been spending money on."

"The toys..."

"Yeah. Their old toys were in pretty bad shape. No child should have old toys."

Alessa ran up to them, smiling. She threw her arms around David's waist. Anna took a step back.

"Hi, David! Is this your wife?"

He smiled. "Yes. Alessa, this is Anna."

"Pleased to meet you," she said and held out her hand. Anna stared at it.

David laughed. "Don't be rude."

She grabbed the girl's hand and shook it.

"You'll have to forgive my wife. She's not used to being around kids." He winked at Anna.

"That's okay. You guys wanna play a game?"

He looked to his wife. She stared at a group of children playing hide and seek.

"Yeah. You go set the board up and we'll be there in a minute."

"Okay!" She skipped off.

"They're... they're so young," Anna said.

"Yeah."

"They look like children."

"They are," he said. "All they want to do is play."

"How...?"

"I don't know. Maybe it's this place. The toys on the wall. I really don't know."

"Do you think other graveyards...I mean...Patrick's grave?"

"No." David shook his head. "I don't." This place was unique in some way. He was sure of that.

He guided his wife to where Alessa and a group of children had set up their game. They sat on the ground next to the board and Anna handed out the pieces. Patrick came over and squeezed in between David and Anna. David looked to his wife and saw a smile on her face. She hugged the boy.

Alessa tugged on Anna's nightshirt. "Can you guys stay here with us?"

Patrick buried his head into Anna's side. "Our parents don't come anymore."

"Little kids should have parents," Alessa said.

David took Anna's hand in his. Pale moonlight caught the tears streaking her face. But she smiled.

The following week, back in their bedroom, David passed a glass of water across the bed to his wife. They kissed and he turned the light off. The dark rushing in no longer felt lonely. Instead it was warm and comforting. It felt *right*.

When their bodies were found, he knew it would be ruled a double suicide. The bottles of pills on the bedside table would give it away if an autopsy report didn't.

Police would never be able to explain the thousands of dollars they had charged at toy stores around Los Angeles or where the toys had gone. The possibility of foul play would be ruled out when security footage revealed the couple paying for the toys, hand in hand and smiling. As he took his wife's hand under the blanket, he was positive anyone watching that footage would see a happy couple and that this would confuse the police even more.

There would be no note found, only a small doll stitched together from a burlap sack, tucked in bed between them.

IL DONNAIOLO

She found Giovanni in the Piazza Navona, sipping coffee with his bitch and waiting out the rain. Amanda stood under the eaves of a closed gelateria and watched through Bernini's Four Rivers. His face was fragile from here, nestled between the Danube's marble triceps and its back. Or was it the Nile? The Baroque had never been her strong suit.

He laughed, crystal eyes catching the moonlight and sparkling like stars. Even if he had been close enough for her to hear, the trickle of rain and the roar of the fountain would have drowned the noise out. But the air vibrated around her, the laugh tickling its way along her skin. It wasn't possible, she knew, but that had been his gift: bringing the impossible to life.

Her phone rang. It was Adam or Jen, wondering where she was. They would be at one of the jazz clubs lining the Campo di Fiori by now with a hundred other students, drinking and dancing until sunrise. She silenced it. What would she tell them? I'm out in the rain and dark, stalking Giovanni?

They had warned her about him. Hell, everyone had warned her about him. *He* had warned her about him. But staying away from him, she always said, would be like not eating if she were starving and someone placed roast boar in front of her.

"Anticipation," he had told her once while kissing her neck, "makes the meal burst with flavor."

In her blood, she knew it was true. That's what this was, she reminded herself. Not stalking, but anticipation.

She wiped a damp hand across her face and tried to focus.

When she looked back toward the café, he was gone.

She stepped into the rain and scanned the piazza. Panic crawled into her stomach. Where was he?

There. By the fountain of Neptune, standing between the god and a dolphin bursting from the water, his body little more than shadow. The girl faced him, back arched, hands braced against the fountain behind her. He brushed the back of his hand down her face.

Amanda bit her cheek. The pain was sharp, and the blood bitter, but all she could think about was how that soft hand felt. How it had been her only a month ago, her dress wet and filthy from leaning against the wall of the Trevi, a thousand tourists chattering and snapping pictures around them as he bent in and the world disappeared.

The rain eased.

His shadow pressed against the girl's.

Amanda's head trembled. Her arms shook.

The rain stopped.

He took the girl's hand and walked south on the Corso, toward the Tiber and then, Amanda knew, on to his apartment.

Her steps clicked on the cobblestone, the noise echoing around her. She stopped by the café and let them walk farther down the alley. She wasn't afraid of losing them. She knew the way.

Two young waiters stood at empty tables and smoked. The harsh smell of their cigarettes mixed with the heady aroma of gnocchi and tiramisu seeping from inside. One of them nudged the other and pointed at her.

"Bella," he said.

The other one nodded. "Scusi?"

His face was young, thin, the features placed in an awkward pattern that suggested he might one day be handsome, but not now. Not while Giovanni's laughing face still burned in her eyes. Bernini would have recognized

Giovanni's hard lines and piercing eyes. This boy would be more familiar to Picasso.

"Yes?" she asked.

"Americana?"

Across the Piazza, Giovanni and his bitch were swallowed by shadows.

"Sì."

The smell grew stronger, more inviting. Would it be so bad to step inside, eat and drink and enjoy the night, and forget Giovanni?

"The blond hair that is short tells me you are. Is not the fashion here." He smiled. "You are a student?"

"I was." She had been studying for her Master's. The test had been two weeks ago back in Boston. She had canceled her flight when Giovanni stopped returning her calls.

"Want to have a seat? We are done with work soon and maybe the three of us will share una botiglia del rosso?"

A bottle of red did sound good right now.

She pictured the cold, black iron frame of Giovanni's bed. The dark satin sheets.

"Non voglio," she said and headed for the Corso.

His cologne lingered in the alley like it had been embedded in the walls. Far ahead two shapes pressed against one another as they walked. Amanda kept a hard pace, the ancient stones sending aches up her calves.

She had met Giovanni on the Spanish Steps. The sun was sinking, the purple sky shot through with veins of orange, as she leaned against the pink brick of the Keats-Shelley house and read Cicero's *On Friendship*. He sat beside her, his smell a sharp musk like he had just been with a woman.

"Poor Chickpea," he said and pointed to the book.

"Why do you say that?"

"He was too much of an idealist, do you not think?"

"I don't know if that's possible."

"Being too much of an idealist?" He looked down where a group of older women laughed at the foot of the stairs, their photo being snapped by one of the Moroccans milling about. "Oh, yes."

He patted her knee and motioned his chin toward the women. She looked down and watched as two small children, no older than five, slipped wallets and cell phones from the women's purses.

"They are idealists," he said, leaning in to whisper. "They want to think no one will take advantage of them here. But this is the Eternal City. It has survived this long because it takes advantage of anyone it pleases."

His voice two pieces of silk rubbed together.

She closed her book. "And me?"

"What about you?"

"Will I be taken advantage of?"

"Oh, most certainly."

They came now to the Ponte Garibaldi and stopped beneath a dull yellow lamp, their shadows long and thin on the bridge's white stones. Giovanni leaned in and pressed his lips against the girl's.

Amanda closed her eyes and pushed her head against the wall hard enough to see stars explode.

The slut took his hand and pulled him away. Why weren't they crossing the bridge? Ponte Garibaldi was his usual route home. He had taken Amanda that way countless times, over the dark Tiber and down into the narrow medieval streets of Trastevere. A few times they hadn't even made it to his apartment, stopping in an alley to grope one another like drunken teenagers.

She followed, sticking to the dark on the opposite side of the street. They must be going to the girl's place. This was likely *her* routine. She no doubt brought men back this way night after night. Some stupid American slut who spread her legs for any man who spoke English with an accent. All anyone had to do was watch the sway of her hips, see how she shoved her breasts against him when she spoke, to see what a tramp she was. Amanda couldn't believe that Giovanni had fallen for it.

That's wrong. She knew he hadn't fallen for it. He was an animal. He had urges. To deny them would have been like denying sleep, or...

Not eating if he were starving and someone put roast boar in front of him.

The soft notes of a violin floated through the streets. She couldn't tell where they came from, but it wasn't a strange sound. There was always music in this city, always some street performer out with his hat. It was one of the things she loved about Rome.

The first night they had spent together a violin played. Teeth clenched, sweat soaking the sheets, the cool breeze rushing down from the Aventine and into his window, wrapping their hot flesh and carrying the sounds of Rome, music and laughter and car horns, as he melted into her, over and over, the night as eternal as the city. They had held one another sometime before dawn. One finger trailed up and down her spine as soft as breath.

She had opened up to him, told him things her closest friends didn't know. She told him about her early years in foster homes, about her adoption, how she wished she knew who her birth parents were. She told him why she really left home, how she didn't understand her adopted mother and was afraid of becoming her.

"Tell me a secret," she'd said, the tears still drying on her face.

He had pulled her close to him, kissed her forehead and ran a hand through her hair. "I cannot have children," he said, his voice hollow and aching. It broke her heart.

There was a comfort in his arms, a vulnerability awakened in her by his kiss, and they had shared far more than their bodies in those few hours.

Giovanni turned down an alley, tugging the girl behind him. She seemed confused, her head darting around. Maybe they weren't going to her apartment after all.

The dark was thick, and the streets twisting, but Amanda was sure they were in the Ancient City. She passed more and more shops displaying tacky T-shirts and gaudy ceramic gladiators in the windows. What were they doing here? There weren't many apartments near the Coliseum.

She followed them out onto the street. They darted across traffic and up the steep staircase of the Campidoglio.

Amanda waited.

Giovanni and the girl disappeared over the hill and into the piazza.

Amanda held her breath and darted across traffic. She crested the hill and stopped when she saw the crowd. Blue light bathed the piazza, washing over the assembly and spilling into the cracks of the marble equestrians guarding the stairs. The hard beat of dance music blasted from speakers lining the square. A stage with white backdrop had been erected across from her, a waif in a thin, silver dress with spiked hair sauntering onto it. The crowd applauded.

Amanda almost wept. It would be impossible to find Giovanni in this crowd. Her eyes flooded and threatened to burst. She refused to cry. Not here, not in front of three hundred strangers. She sucked in a deep breath.

His smell tickled her nostrils. Taunted her. His cologne. His musk. It took her and pulled her past the crowd, behind the museum, and into the brush and broken Roman columns of the Capitoline. It had to be a figment of her imagination. It was impossible to follow someone by scent, especially in such a crowd.

Yet there he was, the girl at his side, stepping down the hill.

He brought the impossible to life.

From the top of the hill the moon burned bright and swollen above Imperial Rome. Trajan's Market stood across the way, its red brick gray in the moonlight like a tombstone for a forgotten world.

She hurried down the hill.

They stood against a wall overlooking the Forum. She inched to the corner of the Mamertine Prison and watched them. Giovanni pulled the girl into an embrace, the moonlight glowing on his skin.

Amanda pressed her hand against the cold stone of the ancient building. Inside, she knew, was a deep dark pit where Rome had thrown her enemies and let them rot. It was too easy to imagine herself in there, weeping in the black and waiting to die.

She fumbled in her purse.

"Never worry about becoming her," he had said once. "Not your adopted mother, not any of them. You will never become what is not already inside you."

The knife was cool in her hand. She squeezed it until her knuckles burned.

The girl leaned back over the wall, moonlight flooding over her breasts and onto Giovanni's face. His hand ran up her thigh, bunching her dress high on the curve of her hip.

Acid burned the back of Amanda's throat.

Anticipation.

Six quick steps and she was with them. The girl's fear was sharp, the smell of beef soaked in vinegar.

The knife slipped between the bitch's ribs, her face a frightened "O." She stumbled back, fell against the stone.

Blood spread out beneath her like wings unfolding.

Amanda dropped the knife. "No... What did I—"

"The hunt," Giovanni said, "must always end in death."

He grabbed Amanda by the back of the head, his fingers knotting in her hair, and shoved her face down toward the wound.

Wheezing breath came from the girl in a weak rhythm. She slumped against the wall, the handle of Amanda's knife standing tall from her ribs, her dress stained and bloody bubbles popping on her lips.

"Look," Giovanni said.

Amanda's breath caught in her throat. Tears burst and ran hot down her cheeks.

The girl's eyes were vacant, glassy, but still managed to burn a hole in Amanda.

Giovanni forced her closer. "See what you've done."

"No," Amanda's voice cracked and small. "God, I'm so sorry, I didn't—"

His scent overwhelming, the musk poured off him in streams. "You did, caramia. You meant it. You hunted her and you killed her."

Below, the ruins of the Forum were painted with thick shadow, the edges tipped with moonlight. Amanda stared into the dark and tried to stop the world from spinning.

His smell crashed over her, the scent of the girl's meat riding it, and her bones trembled. He pulled her closer, his hair falling into her face, and forced her to her knees. The tremor in her bones grew, the joints popping and bulging, and a ripple passed through her flesh like a thousand spider's legs scrambling across her.

Giovanni crouched over the dying girl.

Amanda closed her eyes.

The sound of meat slapping. Fabric ripping. Chewing. Tearing. Slurping.

Low growls. Teeth gnashing. Jaws snapping.

She fought to find her voice. "I didn't want her to... to..."

"I told you, you cannot be what is not already inside you."

The sharp scent of blood hit her, the rancid odor of an open stomach following behind. Giovanni was beside her, his eyes burning, jaw dripping red. He leaned in close, sniffed her throat. She fell against him, crying, shaking, muttering apologies. He kissed her, his taste unmistakable even through the blood.

His tongue darted around her mouth, painting the girl's insides onto her face.

Anticipation.

The girl lay sprawled on the cobblestone, knees akimbo, mouth open, bowels exposed, jagged ribs pointing to the sky. The sight made Amanda's mouth water.

A howl erupted from her throat.

They fell to all fours and dragged the girl into the safety

of the Forum to crack her bones and roll in her blood. The two wolves nipped at one another and licked her mess from each other's fur.

Others watched from ruined temples. As she and Giovanni ate, they crept close, but his growls pushed them back. She was grateful. It was intimate, just the two of them. She was whole. This was passion. Purpose. It was how she felt in Giovanni's bed, pressed against him, the world outside kept at arm's length. She was glad to share it only with him.

He brought the impossible to life.

When she was a woman again, she tried to stand but her body screamed at her. She ground her teeth and took deep breaths, the air cold against her bare skin. She hugged her knees to her chest, the salty tang of meat still on her tongue, and marveled at the blood caked on her.

Around her the cold marble columns and temple walls were rinsed in black. She fought to her feet and sucked in a sharp breath. She hurt, ached all over, but nothing seemed to be broken. She wondered about internal bleeding.

The wind sighed through the ruins. They were out there, she knew. Watching. Waiting for scraps.

She turned to find Giovanni, naked, standing on the steps of the ancient Senate House. The giant green doors were thrown open and a light from inside danced against his skin.

Wolves shuffled through pebbles in the ruins around her.

"They are curious about you." He turned and walked inside.

She glanced back into the dark. The breeze carried an unfamiliar scent, yet strong and heady like Giovanni's. The other wolves crept closer, hovering in the shadows.

She stepped through the doors and into the heart of the Republic. Torches circled the room, their light flickering across the red and green marble floor. White stone seats were tiered around the walls. She stood there, one foot inside, and tried to catch her breath.

"Did you ever think," Giovanni said as he slumped on one of the seats, "when you came to study the Republic that you would ever find yourself here?" He spread his arms and gestured around the room.

Amanda walked inside. Iron grating along the upper walls allowed moonlight to trickle in. A bronze relief of Romulus and Remus suckling at a wolf's tit caught the light from above the door.

"We were kings once," he said, his voice soft and fragile.

She glanced at the others waiting outside the door. "Why does it hurt?"

Giovanni stood and held out his hand. She stepped closer. This close, she could see the blood staining his skin. She fought the urge to taste it, to lick him clean.

"You hurt," he said, "because you let the dream go." He pulled her into an embrace and rocked her back and forth.

The air in the room changed. Soft steps padded around her.

"You don't remember your parents," he said, pulling her to her knees, "because they never existed the way you think they should have."

The other wolves grew closer.

"You are a wolf who dreamed she was a woman."

Soft fur brushed the backs of her legs.

"You let the dream go and tasted that girl with me."

She licked her lips. The blood there was sweet, the taste overpowering. The memory of the girl's flesh, salty with sweat and fear, sent a tremor through her.

Giovanni kissed her. "There are so few of us. We have been waiting for someone like you."

"Like me?"

"Yes." He held her hand against his cheek and closed his eyes.

Hot breath washed over the back of her neck. A wet snout nudged her ribs.

"A bitch in heat," he said.

Her heart fluttered. Tears streamed down her face.

"I love you," she said.

He kissed her hand.

The memory of him pressed against her that first night flooded over her. "I cannot have children," he had said.

He stood.

"Giovanni?"

"For the pack," he said.

He stepped away.

A heavy paw thumped against her back. She submitted, dropping to her stomach. Yellow eyes bored into her. Hot breath carried the odor of rot into her face.

Giovanni was still, silent.

"I'm sorry," he whispered.

His hard, perfect lines formed a beautiful silhouette against the light behind him. If not for his breath, she could have mistaken him for marble.

The weight of the others pressed down on her, their smells tangling together. The sound of the bronze doors closing echoed in the room.

A single tear caught the light as it rolled down Giovanni's face.

The sight broke her heart.

THE PERFECT JACKSON

I was nineteen when we first met the dead man.

We were in a gas station in Wichita when this corpse walked in all putrid, decaying, and dusted in grave dirt. He wore a tattered brown suit and tie, both splotched with mold. Sunken eyes milky. Strands of greasy black hair draped over a mottled skull. A faded "Perot/Stockdale" button pinned upside down on his breast pocket. The smell hit me before the door could even shut behind him.

Raccoon and I had been on the road for a little over a month, stopping here and there to "experience life." Until Wichita, the only things we'd experienced were flat tires, mosquito bites, and dwindling bank accounts. We had felt lost, unsure about the direction of our lives. We were in the midst of a gap-year crisis, one surely inspired by too many pretentious YouTube videos and Instagram accounts. We'd convinced ourselves a cross-country trip would provide the kind of life-changing insight all those *influencers* claimed it did.

After three weeks of looking for that insight, I'd reached the point where every little detail about Raccoon, from his nail-chewing to his horse-like laugh to the annoying way he'd start every sentence with "You know, I've been thinking," made me want to pull off the side of the road and shoot him in the face with a nail-gun. Couple this with the fact that both our money and our pot were running out and it's easy to see just how far morale was dropping. By the time we got to Wichita, we were already talking about turning back.

And then we met the dead man.

When the corpse burst in, I was flipping through the latest issue of *Maxim* while Raccoon microwaved a burrito. The girl behind the counter screamed but the dead man didn't seem to care. Without so much as glancing around, he grabbed the register and slammed it onto the floor. Pieces broke away and went skidding across the tile. Loose change rolled under aisles and cash drifted around the room.

The dead man rummaged through the mess, stopping when he found it.

A single twenty-dollar bill.

He held it up to the fluorescent bulb, eyes without pupils scanning the face of our seventh President. The way the light shined through that old, wrinkled bill it could have been a stained-glass window in the Vatican. It was beautiful. Flawless. A perfect Jackson.

Grinning through rotted lips, he shoved the twenty into his pocket and rushed out the door.

It's important to note here that I generally consider myself a good person. I'm sure everyone does, the odd psychopath excluded. But I had always tried to do right by the general moral code. I avoided lying. I volunteered at my church's soup kitchen every Thanksgiving. And I had never in my life struck someone out of anger. Most importantly, I'd never stolen anything.

Yet standing there staring at the pile of bills on the floor, something whispered in my ear.

He left that for me, it said.

Grabbing cash by the handful, I looked to Raccoon. I didn't need to say anything. He skidded onto his knees and scooped up all the change.

The microwave *ding*ed.

Our pockets full, Raccoon grabbed his burrito and we left.

Outside, the taillights of a truck grew small in the distance.

"That's him," I said.

Raccoon nodded. "Should we follow him?"

To this day, I don't know why Raccoon suggested that. Nor do I know why I agreed. But watching those taillights vanish down a road in Kansas, the setting sun shooting streaks of purple through an orange sky, I had the thought that this was the insight we had been searching for. Here, finally, was that fantastical moment that would change our lives.

Before I could say any of this to Raccoon, sirens wailed from down the road. Sliding into the driver's seat of our beat-up old Camry, I cranked the engine.

"We're criminals now, huh?" Raccoon said.

I pressed the gas pedal, gravel and dust kicking up into the air around us.

"I refuse to let the world label me," I said. "Now shut up and count that money."

We've followed the dead man ever since.

From town to town, he does the exact same thing: runs into a business, smashes a register or rips open a vault, takes a single twenty-dollar bill, and leaves.

We try to be there to take the rest. Sometimes we are. Sometimes we lose his trail and have to read the papers for a week or two to figure out where he's been. It's pretty easy to find him. He's not that subtle.

We've been doing this for two years now. We still have no idea why he does it.

He sticks to the Midwest for the most part, though we have followed him as far as Los Angeles. That was the only time he took more than twenty dollars. Busting into an adult toy store, he left with over two hundred bucks.

We left with four hundred fifty.

That was the one that got our pictures on Fox News. Well, police sketches of us, anyway. The clerk there assumed we were with the guy that busted his register open. It was a reasonable assumption. And true in its own way. We've kept a lower profile since then. As low of a pro- file as possible while knocking over porno shops with a walking corpse, anyway.

The decision had been made somewhere along the way to never think of ourselves as thieves. As I said, we're good people. Simply scavengers. The dead guy is the lion that pounces on his prey and brings it down. We're the hyenas who creep around the kill until the lion leaves. Then we rush in and suck that sweet, sweet marrow from the bones.

It's not a bad life. Beats manual labor.

That's how I felt, anyway.

We're at a taqueria in Santa Fe when Raccoon drops the bomb on me.

"You know," he says, that tiny bit of whine in his voice that appears when he's about to say something I'll disagree with. "Bastien, I've been thinking."

"Yeah? About what?" A piece of quesadilla falls out of my mouth and onto my shirt. Shit. That's gonna stain.

"Well, about this whole thing." He gestures with his hands, some half-shrug thing that I'm sure is supposed to mean our lives.

"What, the taqueria? We can eat somewhere else." I'm not so much joking as I am playing dumb. He's going to have to say it. I'm not bringing it up for him.

"No. This place is good. Reminds me of that place Mom and I used to eat all the time."

Awww. Little Randall Connelly is homesick. Figures.

"I was just, you know, thinking about going home," he says. "Just for a little while."

He stares at his plate, poking his fork into some refried beans. Can't even look me in the eye.

Tossing my silverware onto my plate, I snort. "You wanna ditch me."

"It's not like that. I was just... I don't know. Forget about it." He takes a bite of his beans. Some dribbles from the side of his mouth. He doesn't seem to notice.

Sitting there staring at his sad little puppy dog face, with his stupid Richard Spenser haircut and refried beans dribbling down his chin, I realize just how much I've grown to dislike Raccoon.

No, not dislike.

Hate.

Is that too strong of a word?

I don't think so.

"Maybe it would be good for you to go home," I say. "Just for a while."

A while my ass. Once Mama's Boy is gone, he's dust in the wind.

"You sure?" His face lights up like a kid on Christmas.

It makes me want to head-butt him in the dick.

"Yeah," I say. "I think it would be better for both of us, really. When were you thinking about leaving?"

"Tomorrow, I guess." He's smiling. Absolutely beaming.

"Sounds good. After we eat, I'll take you to the airport to get a ticket. One way shouldn't be too bad this time of year."

Not too bad at all with Mommy's credit card in your wallet, anyway. You sure as hell aren't getting me to pay for it.

"Actually, I was thinking about taking the car."

This little prick. How fucking dare he? What am I supposed to do, drive him? I say this right after it runs through my mind and it comes out just as harsh as I want it to.

"Yeah," he says, ignoring my outburst. "I thought it'd be fun. Go back, visit some old friends. Maybe you could see Rochelle again and—"

"No, no, no. Fucking no. You're flying and I'm staying out here following our lion around. I don't want to see any of our old friends, I don't want to see Rochelle, and I sure as hell don't want to drive all the way back to Knoxville with you. This is my life now and you can just deal with that. Got it?"

"Well, it *is* my car."

Shit. He's got me there.

"Fine. *Fine.* If that's how you want to do it. How much you want for it?"

"Huh?"

"The car. The goddamned car. What do you want for it?"

"Nothing. It's my car. I want to keep it."

"Whatever." I throw the keys at him and stand up. "Take the fucking thing."

I've had enough. If I don't leave now, I think I'm going to hit him.

"Wait! Where are you going?"

"What do you care?"

"Bastien! Wait!"

If he really wanted me to wait, he'd chase after me.

He doesn't and I keep walking.

Stomping down a side-street, I duck into an alley. I'm so pissed off I can hardly stand it. I can't believe Raccoon would just up and leave me like this, all on my own, a thousand miles from home, without even a car. What have we spent the last two years chasing this guy around for, anyway? We're so close to figuring out the dead man's secret, I know it, so goddamned close I can taste the rot.

I'm so angry I could beat the hell out of somebody. Anybody.

I'm so angry I could kill someone.

I'm so angry I sit against the alley wall and cry.

A few hours later, I walk back to our hotel room. Raccoon isn't there and I'm glad. It's pretty obvious when I've been crying. Not much I can do about the puffy, bloodshot eyes or strings of snot that keep dangling out.

Raccoon's stuff is gone. The little shit already left.

I count the cash in my bag and make sure he didn't take more than his share. I know he didn't. Raccoon isn't that kind of guy. But right now, I *want* him to be that kind of guy so I have something else to be angry about. Something to take my mind off how lonely I am.

For two years it's been me and Raccoon. The Dynamic Duo. Even though he annoyed the hell out of me, he was still company. Someone in the same place I was in. Someone who had been touched by our macabre little mystery. Who do I have now?

Just me.

Well. I've still got our lion. Old tall, dark, and rotting. Mister Maggot Bait. Yippee.

Maybe he'll want to go out for a drink after our next robbery?

I'm sure he'd just as soon kill me.

Can he even drink or eat at all? Can he talk?

Hell, can he even *think*? Somehow, I doubt it. He seems rather single minded in his pursuit of the perfect Jackson.

I wonder where he's going to turn up next?

Yesterday, we'd passed his truck on our way into Santa Fe. We knew he was somewhere nearby. The truck was broken down on the side of the road, steam still hissing from the radiator and the passenger side door hanging open.

"That couldn't have happened long ago," Raccoon had said. "Not if there's still water in the radiator."

"What do you know about old trucks?"

He shrugged. "Just seems like the water would eventually get used up. Doesn't it?"

"Hell if I know."

We had pulled up behind the truck on the shoulder of the road. I put the car in park but didn't turn it off. Traffic zoomed by alongside of us.

"Do you think he's still close?"

"No," I said. "Broad daylight and this much traffic? I think he high-tailed it out of here as soon as the truck shit out on him."

We'd sat there in silence, neither one of us fully confident in my assessment.

"Well," I said. "We should check it out before some cop drives by."

"Yeah."

Neither of us moved.

A breeze kicked up and the truck's passenger side door creaked back and forth.

Raccoon had taken a deep breath and exited the car.

The heat would have been unbearable if not for that breeze. My shirt was already soaked with sweat by the time we walked over to the truck.

Raccoon leaned into the passenger seat and I came up behind him. A thick odor hit me and forced me back a step. How the Hell Raccoon could stand being inside the truck, I'll never know. It smelled like some horrible ammonia and rancid beef mixture. Old garbage and roadkill. My stomach churned.

Raccoon just pulled his shirt up over his face and rummaged around.

I stood on the side of the road and watched for passing motorists. When he was done, all he had to show for it was a single twenty-dollar bill.

"What do you think? The perfect Jackson?" He held it up while pulling a twenty out of his wallet. He compared the two and shrugged.

"I doubt it, not if he left it behind." I snatched it from his hands and examined it, hoping to find some clue as to what our lion was up to. The only thing that jumped out at me was the bill's date: 1992. "Where was it?"

"Stuck deep in the crack of the seat." Raccoon had said. The keys were still in the ignition and the glove compartment open.

"He definitely left in a hurry," he'd added.

Today, with Raccoon no longer by my side, I take a look at the green-brown tufts of growth dotting the desert sands. A dead guy on foot couldn't get too far out here. At least I hope not.

Shit. A young slack-ass on foot can't get too far, either. What the Hell am I going to do when the dead man leaves Santa Fe? Some twenty-one-year-old kid with a Tennessee driver's license dropping three grand in cash for a used car might raise some eyebrows.

I need a shower. A nice, hot shower always helps to clear my head. That and some herb. Maybe then I can rev the engine and get a little mileage out of this brain of mine.

The shower manages to dull the anger. Being angry, I've found, is a lot like being drunk. Everything is a little cloudy, thought comes after action, and the details are hard to remember when it's over. At least vomiting isn't one of the symptoms after a night of being pissed off.

Flopping nude onto the bed, I pack a bowl and light up, closing my eyes while I inhale. The stress fades away and my mind becomes clearer. Every thought has meaning. Purpose.

Somewhere deep inside I know this is all bullshit. But does it really matter that I don't actually open my mind up to any great source of cosmic wisdom? I mean, my whole life has been play-acting, hasn't it? High school football for Dad, honor student for Mom, a tepid relationship with that human nasal drip that is Rochelle. If you pretend long enough, you start to believe.

That had always been my problem. Pretending until I believed it. Then when I did believe it, it depressed the living shit out of me. Rochelle wanted me to go to school with her, to hold her hand on the University of Tennessee's campus, to get some fucknut degree that led to some fucknut job so we could get married at her boring ass church and pound out some fucknut kids.

And I smiled and pretended that was what I wanted too, didn't I? Then one day she found me standing on the Henley Street bridge, cars rushing by below, eyes empty and wondering out loud what it would feel like when I crashed through the window of a passing Prius. Three days later, Randall—Raccoon—and I hit the road. I didn't so much as say good-bye.

She didn't deserve that. But what was I supposed to do about it now? Show up on her doorstep with flowers and tell her about the dead man?

Fuck that noise.

The television is droning on in the background, some game show giving way to the local news. The lead story is about a twelve-year old who auctioned a kidney online to pay for his Mom's insulin. The assholes are smiling and talking about how brave the kid is and how this might be the feel good story of the year and all I can think is how much I want to slit my wrists at the idea of a child being forced to sell organs or watch Mommy die.

It's time to assess my situation in the here and now. The key is to put this mystery to bed once and for all. Raccoon took his laptop, as one might expect the little dickbag to do, but I still have his Evernote account linked to my phone. That's where we've made our little clue board, clipping every odd piece of information we've gleaned about our lion in hopes a picture would emerge. None of it amounts to anything. There's no pattern in where he goes. He doesn't leave a wallet or ID behind. He doesn't ever speak to anyone. He just snatches those twenties and hits the road again. It all adds up to nothing.

"George Carl Wagner died in prison today," the TV news anchor says through bleached teeth. "Arrested for the largest armored car heist in New Mexico history, Wagner died of heart failure. It's believed he had an accomplice or accomplices, though Wagner never confessed as to their identities."

I glance up in time to see a photograph of a young Wagner in handcuffs being hauled away by police. He looks like a dipshit, his hair that shaggy bowl cut dipshits wore back then, his coke-bottle glasses reflecting the light of the flashbulbs, his gut straining against his "Perot '92" T-shirt. He looks like what I imagine—

Wait. Perot '92?

The anchor has gone on to tease a charity golf tournament, but Wagner's image is burned into my retinas.

I Google him.

In 1992, it seems, Wagner was a volunteer for the Albuquerque office of Ross Perot's presidential campaign. That office was adjacent to a Wells Fargo distribution center. Police believe he volunteered on the campaign because of its proximity to all those armored cars filled to the brim with cash. In October of that year, just as the activity at the campaign office reached fever pitch, Wagner killed a guard and stole an entire Wells Fargo armored car. The contents were valued at over one million dollars.

By all accounts, Wagner wasn't very bright. He hit the road, disappearing for a few weeks, but then popped up in Missouri, where he purchased a new car (with cash). It was confiscated when he was finally arrested in January of the following year. The remaining money had also been retrieved, nearly eight-hundred-thousand dollars of it, but the three-hundred-thousand-plus Wagner had spent was now in circulation.

And all of it in twenty-dollar bills.

I search for more about the theft, but no additional details present themselves. If he had accomplices, who were they? Where had they gone?

Could our lion have been one?

After an hour, it finally hits me I should search for missing persons in the Albuquerque area from late 1992. The results load just as a thump sounds at the door. Must be a cleaning lady. Didn't I put the *Do Not Disturb* sign out? I thought I did. I should throw some clothes on.

"Give me just a minute."

There's a sharp cracking sound like timber falling and then the door flies open, slamming into the wall. The handle hangs from the door at an awkward angle.

I don't know if he's answering my prayers or my nightmares, but our lion walks in.

No, not our lion. Not anymore.

My lion.

Raccoon is gone. He's just mine, now.

And he's come for me.

He closes the door, jamming it into the cracked frame behind him, and stares at me. I think he's staring, anyway. There are no pupils in his eyes, just a milky white jelly, so it's kinda hard to tell. His mouth hangs open, the muscles of the jaw decayed to the point that he can no longer close it.

A maggot squirms from between his teeth and wiggles its way into a hole in his cheek.

My bladder lets go.

He's come for me. He knows I've been following him, and he's come to kill me. Maybe eat my flesh. That's what walking corpses do, right? Eat warm flesh? Doesn't it ease the pain or something like—

"You've been following me." His jaws creak like a rusty hinge as he speaks. His voice is deep and muffled and sounds like what I imagine tectonic shift to sound like. "You took what wasn't yours."

Ohshitohshitohshit. He's pissed we've been cleaning out the registers and vaults when he leaves. He knows I'm a scavenger. He's going to kill me. I can't die like this. Not naked and covered in urine in some crappy motel in Santa Fe.

He steps over to the bed and I pray I pass out from fear. I don't want to be conscious for this. Just please, please God, let it be quick. Let me pass out and and not feel anything. Please.

I stay conscious. God's a prick.

He grabs my duffel bag and dumps out the contents at the foot of the bed. Cash goes everywhere. He thrusts his hand into a pile and pulls out a single twenty-dollar bill.

Of course! The twenty from his truck. That's what he was after. The one Raccoon grabbed out of the crack in the seat.

Raccoon has just gotten me killed.

Yet another reason to hate him.

The corpse takes the twenty and shoves it into his pocket.

Here it comes. He's gotten what he wanted and now he's going to kill me. Eaten alive like some kind of game animal. I've seen those National Geographic specials about lions killing hyenas. I take one last, long look at him.

That's when I see the bullet hole.

It's the size of a silver dollar in his abdomen. The

shirt there is stained with old blood. The skin beneath is torn open just enough to see inside his abdominal cavity. Things squirm about inside.

Someone shot him in the stomach. But wouldn't the coroner stitch that up?

Not if there wasn't a coroner.

"Wagner," I say.

He cocks his head at that, some approximation of recognition.

"Wagner," I go on, desperate but also excited to have finally pieced it together. "Wagner shot you in the stomach and buried you in the middle of nowhere. He didn't want to split the money."

He doesn't move, still staring my way with his head cocked. He's unnaturally still and I wonder for a moment if he's died again.

"It all makes sense," I sputter. "The twenties. Hundreds of thousands of dollars in twenties. Your share of the robbery. Only Wagner didn't feel like sharing the money, did he? Instead he decided to kill you and keep it all for himself."

The corpse's head snaps forward at that, his chin tucked in and his milky white eyes looking up (I assume) from under his brow in an expression so hateful, so bursting with rage, I'm afraid pissing myself won't be my only embarrassment here.

I swallow and keep going, hoping I can at least prolong my inevitable demise.

"He went into hiding for a while. When he came out of hiding, he went on a spending spree. He bought that car, but God only knows what else. Drugs, hookers, garden gnomes, it doesn't matter. What does matter is he started spending those twenties. Putting them back into circulation where they would end up in gas stations and liquor stores."

He's still. Silent. Maybe trying to determine what to do with me.

"That's what you've been doing, isn't it? You came back for your money. The money you died for. The exact same twenty-dollar bills that cost you your life."

He raises his head slowly...

And smiles.

It's an awkward thing. His dry, rotting skin cracks around the edges of his mouth. Bits of his upper lip split open as it's forced to do something it hasn't done in almost forty years. His teeth, cracked and yellowing, peek through his lips. A small bit of something slimy drips out onto the foot of the bed.

I try to smile back. I don't know if it works or not.

Then, just as fast as he arrived, he's gone.

I shut the door. It doesn't quite fit anymore, so I shoulder it back into place.

What the hell just happened?

I don't know, but I'm alive.

I AM FUCKING ALIVE!

This makes me giggle.

I thought he was going to kill me. Instead I puzzled out his purpose, something we've been trying to figure out for the past two years. Racoon's going to shit a brick when he hears about this.

Except he won't.

Raccoon is gone. It's just me, now.

For the past two years he and I have been following this dead man, delving into his mystery while making a little cash on the side. Now I'm alone and I've solved the greatest puzzle of our lives. What's left? Go back home and tell Raccoon he was right? The trip's over? Time to find some direction?

That thing that just walked out the door was my direction.

I throw some clothes on and grab my bags. I shovel the cash and the rest of my things into the duffel. I throw the backpack on as I grab the door and pull. It's stuck. I pushed it back in too hard.

I plant one foot against the door frame and yank as hard as I can. It flies open, splinters of wood scattering everywhere as I fall on my ass. Get up, Bastien! Get up and hurry your lazy ass down the stairs and into the road!

The tires screech as the car brakes inches from me. The smell of burning rubber fills the air and the driver steps out. For just a moment, silhouetted under the streetlight, he looks regal. Presidential.

Like Andrew Jackson.

"Take me with you," I say.

He smiles that dry, rotting smile of his and tosses me the keys.

"You drive," he rumbles.

Of course. I always drive.

BREATHE

In the space between breaths, I saw her. Gliding across the dance floor, white dress clinging to her curves and flowing behind her like she was submerged, auburn hair cradling a face only Botticelli could have painted, she reached for me, a smile teasing her mouth, crystal eyes moist.

When I inhaled, she was gone.

The music pounding in my head, my third Red Bull and vodka empty on the bar, I thought I'd been hallucinating. Becky rubbed my cheek and asked if I was feeling alright.

"Yeah," I said. "It's nothing."

Three weeks later, the water at Port Hueneme still icy despite the July heat, I saw her again. Underwater she looked the same, only a tear ran impossibly down her cheek to catch in her smile. She almost made it to me before the burning in my lungs forced me to break the surface and breathe. When I went back under, she was gone.

This time I wasn't all right. This time I dove and dove, searching the water for her. Becky couldn't talk me out of the ocean and found a lifeguard to drag me ashore. He accused us of being high and made us leave.

On the drive home, Becky started to cry.

"This is just like before," she said.

"No. It's not. It's nothing like before." Before was horrible. Before was a nightmare I didn't want to relive.

She sniffed and smeared a tear across her cheek. "Are you having an episode?"

An episode. That was what she called it. That was how she referred to finding me curled against the cold porcelain of my toilet, an empty bottle of pills at my feet and a butcher knife in my hand, screaming about the hole inside of me.

"No," I said.

"Then what was that back there?"

I didn't have an answer.

When I dropped her off, she held her arms to her chest and stared at the ground. Her face had gone pale.

"I can't take it if it happens again," she said.

"It won't."

"I know you can't control it but I just..." She couldn't finish. Without looking at me, she kissed my cheek and went inside.

At home, I stared at the ceiling above my bed and finished off a six-pack. The woman I had seen had been real. I knew it the way I knew when I've slept too late. It was tangled worry wedged deep inside and, no matter how I worked at it, I couldn't get it straight.

I took a breath and, for no reason at all, held it.

She was there, drifting from my ceiling like a feather, coming to rest on me. Her dress was cool white satin, her arms even cooler. She weighed so little. The tear rolled from her lips to crash, hot and salty, onto my own. Her eyes took mine and I couldn't look away. Her hands caressed my face and the feel of her against me, of her hair falling around my face and her thighs pressed against my hips, made me whole. Whoever she was, she knew I had been broken, was perhaps broken like me, and we fit together like two statues carved from the same piece of marble. She smelled of lilies and fresh flowing water, smelled of spring, I somehow knew without breathing her in, and before I could inhale to speak her mouth found mine. Her fingers tangled in my hair, her body melting into me, and I could think of nothing but being with her.

When she pulled away, I took a breath.

She was gone.

For the next five nights I lay in bed, holding my breath until my chest ached and my vision blurred, willing her to return. Every night she was there, her mouth instantly on mine, her legs alongside me, our fingers intertwined.

Becky stopped calling after the fourth night of not answering the phone.

On the sixth night as I held my breath, the woman again appeared. She reached down and slid me into her, rocking back to take me inside.

I gasped and she was gone.

Tonight, I'll be ready. With a plastic bag over my head held in place by the tape around my throat, I won't let her go. We'll make love and after, holding each other as I slip into the dark, I'll know that she'll be waiting there for me, waiting in that space between breaths.

IN THE HALLS AND ON THE STAIRS

It starts in the hallway. Staccato steps, faint at first, like the early notes of a Mozart movement, building as more notes are added, the tempo gaining speed. Hard heels crash up the staircase, stomping overhead, before dwindling away. A pause, a beat between pieces, and then back down to pace in front of the bedroom door. Sometimes the knob is bumped and the door shakes in its frame, or the wood is scratched at like a starving dog, but mostly there is pacing.

After what seems like days of huddling under the covers, staring at the door and praying it stays shut, the pacing stops. It doesn't return down the hall, or back up the stairs, but simply stops.

Karen and I went through this for years, from the time our family moved into that farmhouse until each of us left for college. No one else ever heard the steps, not our father or brothers, not visiting cousins. They were just for us.

At Dad's funeral we pulled away from the others and stepped outside to smoke. The service hadn't started yet and our relatives still trickled in from the cold. We walked around the back of the funeral home, snow crunching beneath our boots, as we lit our brands. The gray smoke mingled with our breath to create a fog around us, a blurry haze that looked much the way life does in a dream. It peeled the years from my sister's face like some photographer's gauzy filter and suddenly she was seventeen again, smiling that same sad smile she gave when she left for NYU and told me not to be afraid.

"Dad called me the day before he died." She stared past me, watching cars pull into the lot.

"Me too. He left a message on our machine, but..." I didn't have time for him. It was a hard thing to admit but it was the truth. "Did you two talk at all?"

"For a few minutes, but I was on my way to a date and cut it short."

"Was he...?"

"I knew something was wrong when he called. I just didn't want to deal with it."

"Something wrong like what?"

She took a long, slow drag. Her eyes glistened. "I don't know. It was just his voice. He sounded so... so... alone."

He had been. I don't know how much Karen knew, but the police told Jason he had been dead for eight days before they found him. Eight days. If I go two days without updating my Facebook status people are worried about me. But our father lay on that cold linoleum for over a week before a man from the phone company glimpsed him through the window. If it weren't for a downed line, who knows how long he would have been there? Even his own children couldn't have been bothered to return his calls or wonder how he was doing. There were no friends or girlfriends or neighbors that missed his company during all that time.

My sister had never been one to cry. Even when we were children and one of our pets was found stiff and lifeless, or those steps would sound outside our door at night, Karen had kept the tears inside. But now, almost fifteen years after she left me alone in that house, she wept. I ground my cigarette into the snow and held her. I was shocked at how small her trembling body was, but then I had grown so large in the past few years.

She only gave herself a moment before pulling away and wiping her cheeks.

"I've been thinking about going back to the farmhouse," she said. "There are some things of Mom's I want to grab before the boys sell it all."

Our brothers were practical to an extreme that bordered on cruelty. As soon as the funeral arrangements had been taken care of, they put the house on the market.

No signs had been stabbed into the front yard yet, and no photographs placed on websites, but we had been asked to have anything we wanted out of the house by the end of the month.

"Do you want me to go with you?"

She grabbed my hand. "Would you?"

A horn honked in the parking lot, followed by laughter. Jason and Ben rushed over to our cousin Mike's car, the three of them smiling and embracing.

I sighed. "Isn't it sad families really only get together at funerals? I don't think Mike even came to my wedding."

"Meagan? Would you?"

"Yeah. Sure." In my mind, the sound of heels on a hardwood floor echoed. "Do you have a hotel?"

"No. I thought..." She bit her bottom lip and squeezed my hand.

I had been thinking it too. "I think the power's still on. Besides, I doubt I'll feel like driving straight back to Chicago after all of this."

She finished her own cigarette and tossed it into the snow. "Chris won't be expecting you?"

"I'll call him. He won't mind. He's probably sick of rubbing calamine all over Julie, but I think he can last another day."

"Is she all right?"

"Just chicken pox. He thought it'd be better if he stayed to take care of her. The drive would have been hell if we had brought her with us."

Jason waved from the parking lot.

"I guess we're starting," I said.

Karen gripped my hand again and we walked, like children, inside.

My station wagon crunched over gravel as it made its way up the hill. Since we were kids each of us had nagged Dad to pave the driveway, but he never did. He was a simple man, not really belonging to this age, and never truly chose to participate in the modern world. We would find no computers in the house, no cell phones, no energy-efficient bulbs. The most modern thing would be the microwave Chris and I had bought him for his birthday six years ago. He always complained about it, griped about how it dried his food out and made the meat rubbery, but he still used it for almost every meal. A man on his own cannot argue too much with convenience.

The thought of my father sitting down by himself to a microwave dinner in this large, silent house brought fresh tears.

I parked the car and waited. The headlights colored the grass leading to the house and shined back from the large window of the living room. Thick, purple drapes hung closed inside. My imagination, already humming from the moment Karen mentioned coming here, filled in the shadowy presence lurking behind the cloth, pacing back and forth, daring us to enter.

Her SUV skidded to a stop next to me. I killed my engine and stepped from the car while my sister clicked on her interior light and rummaged around for her things.

When she stepped out, she laughed. "I had this stupid idea you would chicken out and leave me here all alone tonight."

"Why would I do that?"

Even though she had done it to me, left me here for over a year by myself in that room while the steps marched outside my door.

The mat at the kitchen door was frozen to the concrete. A strong tug ripped it away, shards of ice flaking off onto the key hidden below it. Jason had always joked that anyone could get into the house if they wanted to, that there had to be a better hiding place, but Dad would just shrug and say, "Who the hell would want to come in here?"

I dusted the ice away and slid it into the lock.

We were both quiet as we stepped inside and flipped

on the light. My guess is the same fear gripped Karen that had hold of me, that I had been wrong, and the power had already been turned off, but the bulb flared to life.

A chair lay on its side next to the kitchen table. I couldn't force my eyes from the linoleum around it.

That had to be the spot where he died.

The wind whistled outside, the house creaking like old bones forced to move while we stood motionless in the doorway.

Karen nudged the door shut and sat her bag on the table. She grabbed the chair, pulled it upright, and slid it into position. She undid the buttons on her long coat and shrugged it off, draping it onto the chair and hiding the thing from sight.

I could see why she had kept the coat on throughout the service. Her black dress hugged every curve of her body. She had felt so small in my arms earlier but now, looking at her thin frame sculpted to perfection through long hours of running and Pilates, I was jealous. She did not have the flesh I had collected around my hips. Her ass and breasts had not been defeated by gravity the way mine had. Skin did not hang like wings from her arms.

She sat opposite her coat. "Feels weird, doesn't it?"

"So empty."

"Did you call Chris?"

"Yeah. He says 'hi.'"

"Oh?"

"So does Julie. She asked if you were ever going to come and visit."

"Uh... sure. Yeah. Maybe not soon—work's so crazy I barely got here today—but definitely as soon as I can."

"Or maybe we can bring her up to New York. Chris gets sent to Jersey so much for work, might as well make a weekend of it sometime."

"Oh. Chris goes to Jersey?"

"Yeah. Some plastic company there is one of his big clients."

I found a box of black tea in the cabinet, probably left over from the last time I'd visited, and we sipped from steaming mugs while avoiding the topic of our childhood.

It was Karen who eventually brought it up. She had always been stronger than me.

"Do you think we'll hear it tonight?"

I stared past her into the dark of the living room, acutely aware that neither of us had made it any farther into the house than where our father had died. "I hope not."

"Did you ever wonder...?"

"What?"

"I don't know. It seems so silly to talk about it now." The way her eyes glanced to the ceiling and her hands trembled, she found it anything but silly.

"Go on."

"Did you ever wonder if it was Mom?"

"It wasn't Mom."

"How can you be so sure?"

"Those steps are loud. Hard. The steps of someone much larger than Mom. And angry. Whatever it is, it's so angry. Can't you feel it?"

She shrugged. Neither of us mentioned how I had just spoken of the steps in present tense.

"Besides," I went on, "if the footsteps were Mom's, why couldn't Dad or any of the boys hear them? Why just us?"

"Maybe she had something to tell us."

"Like what?"

Karen didn't have an answer. I sipped my tea and stared into the black, eyes straining to trace the shapes of furniture tucked away there. When was the last time any of us had been here? Last Christmas? None of the boys had made it, but we had driven in that morning and spent all day here. Chris had talked to Dad about how hopeful they were for the Cubs next season and Julie sat at the table and watched me cook dinner. Karen had stopped by for most of the day on her way to see some old friends. After dinner, Julie sat on my lap and listened to Dad read "A Christmas Carol" while Chris and Karen sat outside, drinking eggnog and smoking. They had been close since college, Karen being the one who set us up on our first date, and I never thought anything of the time they spent together.

None of us stayed that night. Neither Karen nor I had spent the night since moving out.

Until tonight.

"Shall we?"

She took a deep breath. "No time like the present."

We grabbed our bags and hurried through the living room, pausing on the staircase to flip the light on. When we reached the second story landing, Karen shuffled over to our room.

"You coming?"

The dark of the third-floor bled shadows onto the staircase. There were thirteen steps up to that floor, an unlucky number memorized from every errand I'd ever ran to the junk room Dad had made up there. Now, staring into nothingness, the hairs on my arms and neck struggled to free themselves. What was waiting for me there, hiding above those thirteen steps, glad I had come home?

"Meagan?"

"Sorry."

Our room was just as we'd left it. Karen had taken some of her posters down and snatched her desk lamp when she left for college, but the furniture was still in place. My posters were tacked to the wall, welcoming me back in the language of late-nineties pop culture. Our beds were made. The drapes hung closed. The dry smell of books and cardboard boxes filled the air, that smell of long gathered dust being disturbed. It reminded me of warehouses and old libraries. A few more steps awakened the gray scent of mildew.

We paused, reminded of all the years we had been away.

"I'll open the window and let it air out."

Karen nodded and leaned over her bed. She sniffed the blanket. "I don't think it's our beds."

"It's the drapes," I said, pulling them aside to fight the

window open. Their white had turned to a dull, splotched color.

"We should probably just take them down." She marched over and yanked them from their hooks.

The window screamed up its track. Frigid air rushed in to fill the room. Karen shivered when she returned and pulled her coat back on.

"I put them on Jason's bed," she said.

"Should air out in just a minute." I almost suggested sleeping in a different room, but neither of us wanted that. As frightened as we were, I think we needed to hear those steps, to be assured they were real, and all our sleepless nights hadn't been in vain.

She dug through her bag and emerged with a tiny black case. "Hang out with me while I wash my face?"

"Sure."

In the bathroom, she spread the contents of her case out onto the cold porcelain: toothbrush, toothpaste, face wash, moistener, eye cream, cold cream, and an exfoliating cleanser.

"I didn't even bring a toothbrush," I said.

She winked at me and pulled an unopened twin pack from her case. "Be prepared. That's the Boy Scout motto."

I tore the packaging open. "And why do you know that?"

"I dated a Scout leader once. Turn the heat on."

The heater roared to life. Through the vents in the ceiling it glowed yellow then red and soon scalding dry air showered us.

I lowered the toilet seat and sat. "Seeing anyone now?"

Karen lathered one of her concoctions in her palms. "Uh... yeah. Kind of."

"Kind of?"

"Well, it's just something fun. It's not going anywhere."

"You have a lot of those."

"Don't I know it." She applied the foam to her face with the precision of a mason spreading mortar. "Can I ask you something?"

"I don't know. I'm always suspicious when someone

asks if they can ask me something."

"I just... Well, you and I have never talked about it, but I always wondered..."

"Spit it out."

"Do you ever regret dropping out?"

Almost every day, I thought. I had finished my Bachelor's degree and took a couple of years off to work before going back for my Master's. Then I met Chris and things had moved so fast. Not long after moving in together, his job pulled him to Chicago. I followed, planning to go back to school the next fall. The following year we were married. Then came Julie. One day I woke up and realized all of my dreams had somehow drifted away.

"Never," I said. "Not one bit."

"That's good. I think I always envied that about you."

"What?"

"The family stuff. I sometimes wish that was enough for me, that I was happy just settling down with the right man and having kids."

Enough? I almost asked but didn't.

After our evening rituals (hers much more complicated than mine), we closed the window and cranked the heat in own room. She slipped into a T-shirt and sweatpants while I dug through some of Jason's old gym clothes from a box in his closet. Soon we were nestled under our covers, blanketed in the smell of cotton and youthful fantasies. We were kids again, the night light burning in the corner, whispering to each other over the space between our beds as though anyone were in the house to hear.

Sometime not long after midnight, we fell asleep.

"Meagan. *Meagan.*"

I rolled over to face her. Sleep blinked away in three agonizing seconds. She was upright in bed, her knees pulled to her chest.

"What?"

"I think it's started."

My heart pounded. I sat up. The dull light in the room groped at the walls. The door was rimmed in black.

"I don't hear any—"

"Shh."

My ears strained in the silence.

Was that footsteps?

It was hard to tell. The wind blew outside. A branch scratched against the side of the house. The wood creaked. Karen's mattress squeaked with every shift of her weight. Our breath was paced, measured. My heartbeat in my ears.

Down the hall, something tapped against the floor.

Karen leaped from her bed and forced herself into mine. "See?"

There was another tap. Soon another. It didn't take long before footsteps pounded down the hall and up the staircase. They paced overhead, back and forth. A long silence, and then the floor above us creaked as though someone shifted from foot to foot.

"Oh, shit, Meagan. We didn't lock the door."

As if hearing her, the steps pounded back to the staircase.

I was out of bed before I knew what I was doing. Sweat pasted Jason's shirt to my back as I sprinted across the room. It was a race, my heavy feet stomping in time to the heels rushing down the stairs, my heart rattling in my chest, so very afraid of what would happen if I didn't reach that door first.

The lock slid into place. I exhaled, not realizing I'd been holding my breath the entire time.

A loud thump sounded on the floor. The doorknob rattled.

I wrestled back under the covers. The door shook. Steps marched back and forth. They made it all the way to Ben's room before returning to our door.

When the scratching started, Karen screamed.

Breakfast was eggs and bacon, with a giant pot of coffee we had to drink black because the milk had gone sour. We were quiet while eating, our eyes circled in purple like raccoons. When we finished, I gathered the dishes and rinsed them in the sink. It struck me this might be the last meal anyone in our family ate in this house.

"What did you want to get of Mom's?"

Karen yawned, stretching her hands overhead. "Her jewelry, mostly. Thought one of us should get it instead of April."

Our sister-in-law had the annoying habit of scavenging any rings or clothing she could get her hands on.

"I'd like to get the Christmas ornaments," I said. "Especially the ones she got from Grandma."

Karen nodded. "You should. Julie would like those."

"Wanna smoke first? I'm still a little too tired to—"

"Shhh." Her eyes went wide.

"What?"

Then I heard it too.

A tap.

"It can't do that," I said. "It's never happened if we weren't asleep and—"

Another.

Overhead, the heels clicked over the floor. If I looked around the corner then, looked up the staircase to the second-floor landing and farther, up those thirteen steps to where it always paused, I would see whatever stomped through the house.

The steps sounded on the staircase. On the third floor it went quiet.

Karen climbed from her chair.

"What are you doing?"

"Hush."

She crept to the corner. The steps tapped their way back down the stairs. She froze, her face inches away from a clear view all the way to the third floor.

She couldn't look, and I was glad.

The footsteps paced above us.

Her face was pale as she turned back into the kitchen. We stood silent. I fought to breathe, afraid the steps would find their way down the stairs this time.

Our bedroom door banged hard against the wall.

It's in our room, Karen mouthed.

I couldn't move. We waited.

Silence settled into the house, the pressure easing as though someone had left the room. It was gone again.

"I need a smoke." My hand trembled on the doorknob.

Karen was behind me before the door opened.

The view outside was of a blank, soiled canvass. White ground rose to meet gray sky, the line separating the two as faint as our breath in the freezing air.

Karen's phone vibrated in her pocket. She pulled it out, her thumb tapping away on the keyboard with the rhythm of those steps. Seconds later, my own phone buzzed. It was Chris, wondering when I would be home. I texted back to say I'd call him later.

"Thank you for coming with me." Karen pressed her hand against my arm.

We went through several more cigarettes before working up the nerve to go back inside. We held hands as we climbed the stairs.

Our bedroom door yawned open.

We crept inside.

"Nothing's been disturbed," I said.

Karen ran a hand across her face. "Let's keep it locked from now on, even when we're not in it. Okay?"

"Yeah."

She double-checked the lock when we exited. Halfway down the stairs she put a hand on my shoulder.

"Hold on," she said.

She ran back up the stairs and checked the lock again.

We spent the afternoon rummaging through dressers and the junk room upstairs. Our mother's jewelry was kept in a lock box in Dad's closet. Photo albums were stacked next to it and we divided them. The Christmas ornaments were on the third floor, right next to where the steps always paused, stuffed in between Jason and Ben's old sporting gear, baseball bats and football pads crushing the edges of the box down but not damaging any of the glass inside.

When we had loaded our cars with what we wanted, Karen closed her trunk. She stared up at the house and drew quick, hollow breaths.

"We'll never see this place again," she said.

I drew her into my arms, and we cried.

"Why don't we take hot showers and make one last sweep of the place? Then we can get burgers down in Lewiston before hitting the road. What do you say?"

She nodded and shuffled inside.

I lay on my childhood bed, its familiar lumps and odor all around me, and called Chris. The call went straight to voicemail, which meant his phone was off or he had ignored me. Either way I told him I would be leaving soon, that I missed him and Julie so much and couldn't wait to be back home.

Karen was still drying her hair as she walked into the room. "How long you think you'll be in the shower?"

"Maybe twenty minutes?"

"I'm gonna take a nap before we head out. Wake me when you're done?"

"Okay."

"I'm gonna shut and lock the door. Just in case."

"Did you put the key back on the frame?"

"Yeah."

I ran my fingers along the top of the door, my nails scratching over dust covered wood until I felt the tiny key we had always hidden there.

Karen locked the door and I headed into the bathroom. Steam clung to every corner, pressing my hair to my neck and painting the mirror in the same dull gray of the sky. My sister had left her black case on the sink, the contents still on display. I packed them up for her.

Her cell phone blinked from the counter. She really must have been exhausted. The consummate business-woman never let it out of her sight.

Steam wiped away from the mirror with a few swipes. Cotton-edged streaks shot across in places, breaking my reflection into smeared edges.

Her phone buzzed again. I glanced down. The screen read *2 New Messages*. Wondering if they were important enough to wake her, I clicked *VIEW*.

They were both from Chris. He was always so worried about me. Probably checking with my sister to see how I had handled the funeral. The newest one was just one word: "Well?"

I scrolled to the first message, received fourteen min-utes earlier, around the time I had tried to call him. It read: "Aftr Meg gets back mayb I get calld 2 NJ again 4 few days. B good 4 both of us. I need u."

The phone hit the floor with a dull tap, bouncing once before a tiny sliver of glass fell from the screen and skid-ded away.

Connections formed. No, that's wrong. They had always been there, little snippets of conversation and strange vague discussions and the timing of business trips and late-night calls and my sister on the porch with my husband at Christmas and a hundred other little things I hadn't wanted to see, that I had kept locked away behind closed doors until now.

The tears came hard, doubling me over, fighting my lungs. Hands on knees, stomach convulsing, skin hot as death. The room spun.

I stumbled into the hall, toward our room, vision blurred and heavy, wheezing breath filling my ears. What would I say to her? I wanted to stop crying, wanted to be angry, wanted to be in control for one goddamned moment of my life.

The rail was cold in my hand. I squeezed it so hard fighting up the stairs, feeling as though I was falling, falling upward, squeezed it so hard splinters bit into my palm. My knees struck the floor in front of the window, the cold afternoon light slapping me in the face for the fool that I'd been.

Behind me I thought I had heard the echo of footsteps, but I didn't care if they were mine or not. My world was nothing but sharp tears of glass ripping into my face and stabbing me in lungs wet with the blood of my happy suburban lie.

I don't know how long I sat there, crying, rocking back and forth like I was a little girl with a skinned knee who just needed her father to sweep her up in his arms. But my father was dead, had died on the linoleum two floors below, cold and alone. My husband was no longer mine, gone the way hopeful words vanish into the air after they're spoken.

I had nothing.

Yet my sister...

My sister who had left me alone. My sister who was always prettier, always smarter, who had carved her own path while mocking me for mine, who had kept the shape any man would still want, who had seduced my husband out from under me. When? Last Christmas? Earlier? Did it matter?

My brother's Louisville Slugger felt good in my hands. It felt solid in a way nothing else did.

She yelled from behind her door as I came down the stairs. "Meagan! Get in here! The steps are—"

"Shut. Up." I marched over.

"Is that you?"

I could almost see her cowering on the bed, afraid of ghosts. My hip crashed into the knob as I passed, red thoughts clouding my head, overfilling it until it threatened to burst. The curtains were spread out over Ben's bed. Maybe I should just lie down? Maybe go into Ben's room and call Chris and talk about how my world had ended in one brutal moment?

Instead I spun, gripping the bat tight until veins stood on the backs of my hands.

In front of the door, I remembered it was locked. I scratched around the frame, groped for the key. Karen screamed.

"Meagan! Is that you? You're scaring me."

The key slid into the lock. The door crashed against the wall hard enough to send it back into me, bouncing from my shoulder. The sounds echoed in my ears—the steps, the scratching, the doorknob—and I knew then what we had been hearing all these years.

Karen's eyes, so much like a child's, were white with confusion.

The bat sliced through the air, ending her with the hard crack of firewood splitting.

The steps, I know, will sound no more.

THE SCOTTISH PLAY

Every theatre has a ghost.

I've done Mamet Off-Broadway, Beckett in London's East End, and Noel Coward at a community playhouse in Alabama. From Chicago to Edinburgh, what all those theaters had in common, other than miserable directors and bad lighting, were their ghosts. Chalk it up to throwing a group of people with overactive imaginations into a dark building for nights on end, but I have yet to visit a theater that wasn't reputed to house the dead.

In two-thousand-three, we leased a ninety-nine-seater off Santa Monica Blvd in Los Angeles. "Theater Row," the area's called. Our building was a non-descript beige box, a chain link fence drifting from one corner to surround a ten-space parking lot. From the outside, without the banners and posters and makeshift marquee, it could have been mistaken for a dentist's office.

The lobby was cozy, a burgundy sofa against one wall and a ticket counter against the other. Past the ticket counter, double doors painted to masquerade as cherry wood opened onto a small landing crowded with blue seats and the dry scent of old paper. The next few rows spilled downward until stopping before the stage. It was small but adequate, a simple concrete floor painted cobalt, chips here and there revealing the black underneath.

Our ghost was named Sydney. If a cool breeze kicked up some papers or someone heard a strange noise, it was blamed on him. The story was that Sydney was a silent film actor who, after failing to make the transition to talkies, hanged himself in the house that used to sit on the spot.

Sydney was said to be a playful ghost, kind-hearted and happy simply to be noticed.

This story is not about Sydney.

Peter and I loved the place. We named it "Theatre Obscura" and planned to put rising talent to work before they were snatched up by soap operas and cat food commercials. We had a great group that first year and performed everything from *Ten West* to *Noises Off*. Opening night was always sold out.

To congratulate ourselves, Peter and I took a honeymoon at the end of the year. We weren't really married (this was years before that issue even hit the courts) but had been together for almost a decade and thought it deserved something special. The plan was to start in Italy and make our way north to the village in Scotland where Peter's grandparents were born. It was to be a calm and relaxing break from the pressures of running a business. And it was, up until we phoned the theater from Brighton to check on things.

"What do you mean, 'cease and desist?'" Peter scratched his scalp. "Uh-huh. And why the hell did you do that? I see." When he hung up the phone, we ordered two pints of lager and took a corner booth at the pub.

"Well?"

He sighed. "James, we have been blacklisted from the Dramatist's Playbook."

"What? That's ridiculous. Why would we—"

"Because Terry, that miserable fuck, decided to make Estragon a woman."

"Has he ever read *Godot*?"

"It seems he has not." He sucked down half of his lager and wiped his mouth. "They received a cease and desist letter that he neglected to tell us about and which he promptly ignored. Now we have been denied access to half of all of the plays out there."

Terry was an ambitious director who, unfortunately, lacked the talent and vision that he told everyone he had.

We'd left him in charge of a production of *Waiting for Godot*, the *Hamlet* of modern theater, while we were gone. When acquiring the rights to produce a play, the playwright often has stipulations that go along with it, choices the director is allowed to make and choices they aren't. The Samuel Beckett estate does not allow a change in gender of the characters or rewriting of any dialogue. And yet Terry, who we had spoken to before about his penchant for "stunt casting," had decided to flaunt those prescriptions and violate the contract we had signed.

The punishment was devastating. Being blacklisted from the Dramatist's Playbook could potentially cripple the theater. It would mean the inability to stage a majority of the plays out there. Terry had pissed all over our grand little enterprise to stroke his own ego.

"We have to fly back," David said. He downed the rest of his beer and slammed the mug onto the table. "Goddammit."

The other patrons glanced at us and went back to their business.

"I'll go," I said.

"Huh?"

"I'll go. I'll take the train to Heathrow tomorrow morning and you can head up to Scotland."

"I can't ask you to do that."

I took his hand. "I want to. I couldn't forgive myself if you came this close to seeing where your family's from and then were taken away."

"Are you sure?"

"Positive."

His smile was worth the fee the airline charged for changing my ticket.

Back in Los Angeles, my first task was to fire Terry. He didn't take it well.

"You can't fire me." Terry was a large man with arms like timber.

"I can and I have. Please leave."

"You little cocksucker," he said, shifting his weight

between the balls of his feet and flexing his fingers.

I was afraid he was going to hit me. I'm sure he would have, if the cast hadn't been there at the time.

Someone jumped up at the sound of the "c" word, but Terry was gay, and I didn't flinch. He had always made jokes about how effeminate Peter and I were, as though our slight frames and fondness for musicals made us negative stereotypes. Perhaps we were stereotypes, but at least we had some kind of talent.

He stared at me, nostrils flaring, before glancing around the room at the others. He tossed his script at my face and stomped from the theater, smacking the double doors hard enough on the way out to rip one from its bottom hinge.

I spent hours over the next week groveling to both the Beckett estate and the Dramatist's Playbook. I managed to avoid a lawsuit but couldn't regain immediate access to their plays. We were put on a "one-year suspension," meaning that for the next twelve months we couldn't perform anything that would actually put butts in the seats.

"Fine," Peter said when I told him over the phone. "We can work with that."

"How?"

"We'll do Shakespeare."

"Shakespeare. In Los Angeles?"

"Why not? Shakespeare has everything. Sex, violence, the occult."

"The occult?"

"Yeah. Why don't we do *Macbeth*?"

"Shhh! Don't say that. I'm at the theater." That particular work of the Bard's is cursed. As legend goes, muttering its title inside a theater will doom the production to tragedy. Actors simply refer to it as "The Scottish Play" as a result.

Peter laughed. "You know, I'm only about ten miles away from his castle."

"Whose castle?"

"Macbeth's."

"Glamis Castle? Really?"

"Yeah. Listen, why don't you hold auditions and I'll direct it when I'm back?"

"I don't know..." I wasn't into the idea for a number of reasons, the curse being only one of them. But Peter had a gift for whittling down my resolve to nothing. Before I had even agreed to it, I knew the only way the conversation would end was with me rolling over and giving in.

We found our cast and Peter came home to direct. I picked him up at LAX and drove straight to the theater for the table read. He threw the doors open, tossed his luggage to the ground, and leaped onto a chair with the type of energy that made me fall for him in the first place. The actors laughed and stared up at him, eyes wide, waiting for some grand speech.

Peter pulled a leather pouch from his pocket and tossed it onto the table.

"What's that?" Banquo asked.

"That," Peter said as he stepped down and sat, "is earth from MacBeth's grave."

Someone gasped, whether at the grisly trophy or mention of the name I'm not sure.

Lady MacBeth poked it with a pen. "Really?"

"Indeed, it is," Peter said. "Or close enough to it. I just returned from Scotland where I had the misfortune of visiting Glamis Castle. While there I stole a handful of dirt from the cemetery."

This was par for the course with Peter. He had stolen dirt from Caesar's grave in Rome, from the amphitheater in Pompeii, and from the grounds of a thirteenth century monastery in France. It was his alternative to photographs. Pagan, in a way, but he had spent his entire life in the theater. It was impossible not to develop eccentricities.

Everyone made the prerequisite jokes about how morbid it was, about the curse, and about Terry's *Godot* ("Waiting for Godawful," one of the witches said), and then the table read started. I left them to it and went to the office to crunch numbers and plan our promotional strategy.

Our office was located behind the stage. To reach it, you had to enter through a door behind the box office and walk down a long, narrow hallway spanning the length of the theater. At the end of the hall you could take a left to go backstage, a right for the bathroom, or head straight into the office. There were two red lights hanging midway through the hall, dull bulbs that barely kept us from ricocheting off the cramped walls. We kept the door to the office open and a lamp burning inside like a lighthouse.

This time, the hallway was dark aside from the dim red glow. The office door must have been closed. I flipped through my keys, searching for the key to the office. The booming voice of our Scottish Lord sounded through the wall.

Two heavy footsteps stomped in front of me. I looked up, expecting to see Peter or one of the actors.

The hallway was empty. The door to the office wide open. The lamp on.

For an instant, I thought I had seen someone standing in front of the door, someone large enough to block the light. I thought of Terry and my stomach knotted.

The shadows shifted, that's all. I shrugged it off and went to work.

After the table read, when we were locking up, Peter asked what I thought.

"I didn't watch it. I had too much work to do. I was in the office for most of the play."

"No, you weren't."

I laughed. "I think I know where I was."

"You were sitting in the back row. I saw you."

"You didn't see me."

"I saw someone."

I mentioned the footsteps in the hallway.

Peter frowned. "We should give the place a once over

before locking up." There are scores of homeless on Santa Monica and we've had to escort more than a few from the theater. We searched every room, every storage area and crawlspace, but the theater was empty.

"Maybe it was someone who came with one of the actors," I said. "A boyfriend or roommate or someone."

"Must have been." He didn't sound so sure.

We locked up and went home.

That was to be my one strange experience at the theater. Two days later I slipped while walking through the rows of seats and fell down the stairs. I fractured my leg in three places and was confined to home for the bulk of the production. On the way home from the hospital, I joked that it was Peter 's fault for saying the title aloud.

Luckily, most of the work I needed to do could be accomplished from my laptop and Peter hired a student named Nikki to act as stage manager in my place.

Peter was at the theater day and night. This was typical when he directed a production. He lived in the space and, while I missed him, I didn't think much of it.

"Sydney came to watch us again," he said one night while crawling into bed.

"What?"

"We saw the figure in the back row again today. I ran to see who it was but, when I got there, the seat was empty. The cast thinks it's Sydney."

This became a standard nighttime greeting during the Scottish Play. It seemed Sydney was a big fan.

As rehearsal went on, Peter would come in later and later, his skin ashen, his eyes surrounded by sagging purple. Coughing fits would wake him in the middle of the night.

"You're running yourself ragged," I said over breakfast one morning. "Slow down."

"I'm fine. I've just caught a cold is all."

I wasn't so sure, but I knew Peter well enough to know his pattern. While the play rehearsed, his life would be consumed by it. Once it went up and no longer needed so much of his time, he'd relax and take care of everything he let slip, including his health. Doctor appointments were never made until a show was on its feet.

On the night of dress rehearsal, Peter never came to bed. I woke around three in the morning to find him in the living room, a bottle of Scotch in one hand and the television remote in the other. The television was on some reality show, the bare breasts of an orange skinned woman covered by a blurred bar and the volume muted. The blue glow cast harsh shadows against Peter, and I was shocked at how horrible he looked. Seeing him every day, I hadn't noticed until that moment just how much weight he'd lost recently.

"Are you okay?"

He turned the television off and leaned back in his chair. "I don't know."

I sat on the sofa next to him and took his hand. We were quiet for a long while.

He took a deep breath and asked, "Do you think I'm off?"

"Off?"

"Crazy."

"No. Why would I think that?"

Eyes quivering, lips pressed tight, he nodded. "Alright. Alright."

"What happened?"

He stared at our hands wrapped together. Closing his eyes, he told me what had happened. If it had been any-one else, I would have thought they were crazy. But Peter wasn't afraid of anything and, while he was imaginative and eccentric in many ways, he was never naïve and rarely superstitious.

That morning, he said, he had gone to the theater early. He was at the computer, sifting through emails, when he heard the double doors bang open. His breath caught in his throat. It was too early for Nikki to be out of class and, aside from me, no one else had keys to the theater. Heart pounding, skin hot as fevered death, he couldn't understand why he was so anxious. The air was alive, he said, and even telling me what had happened I could see sweat beading on his arms. The energy in the theater was the nervous fear that filled dressing rooms before a performance: expectant, hesitant, pregnant with anticipation.

A prop sword leaned against the desk. He gripped it tight, his knuckles white, and stepped onto the stage.

It was quiet, the low rumble of the air conditioner the only sound. The house lights were dark, and a single lamp rinsed the floor of the set. He marched up to the double doors and propped them open.

The lobby was empty.

He double checked the lock on the front door and, satisfied that it was in place, made his way back down the long hall, convinced he had misinterpreted a noise from the alley behind the theater. He went back to the computer and replied to an email. The smell of wet earth drifted into the office and he worried the air conditioning was about to go.

There was a sound at the end of the hallway.

He stopped typing and listened.

It happened again, a soft scratch against the wall. Rats, he thought, and made a note to call an exterminator.

The scratching grew loud and frenzied, the sound of claws scrambling over the ground. It reminded him of when our terriers would race across the hardwood floors, their claws unable to gain traction. He grabbed the sword again, afraid that a massive rat made its way toward him.

He stared into the shadows swirling in the hall, split and punctuated by the dull red lights, expecting to see something the size of a tabby racing his way. The scratching continued, the claws slipping, scrambling to regain footing, pulling the thing along through the black.

It broke into a pool of red cast by the backstage lights. Much larger than a dog, it was closer to the size of a human torso. He described it as shadow pulled into shape from its place on the wall, a rustling, roiling black that caved in like an empty coat in the center, long arms like gnarled tree limbs twisting before it, rapidly pawing at the ground to pull it along.

He slammed the door and leaned against it. A thud hit like a fist, its weight rocking him, and the scratching continued at the door. The smell of wet earth clogged his nostrils, the scent of moldy damp cloth riding along with it. Peter couldn't breathe, couldn't think, could only lean against the door, eyes shut, sword gripped tight to his chest, praying that it would leave, would drip back into whatever grime filled hole it had crawled from.

The scrambling climbed the door. It hit the ceiling and he could hear it scratch and paw and fight its way back down the hall from above, slipping back into the black and eventually, thankfully, going silent.

He slid down the door and sat there for an hour, his back pressed against it like a blockade, waiting for Nikki to come and let herself in. He played it off when she did, pretended he had taken a nap in the office, and told himself it was nerves, that the stress of everything was getting to him. He resolved to take a break when the play was done and not to mention the incident to anyone, even me.

Especially me, I suspected, and felt guilty for it.

I ran my finger along his arm. Damp with sweat, I expected it to be hot. Instead it was cool, like leather in the fall.

"Jesus, Peter." He held up a hand, the same gesture he made when giving direction and an actor began to ask questions.

He had always hated to be interrupted, hated to let his mind slip from wherever it was.

I was quiet.

He sucked in a trembling breath and continued.

After the dress rehearsal, he found himself alone in the theater again. Nikki had to leave by ten to pick a friend up from the airport and the rest of the cast wanted to get a good night's sleep before returning the next morning for one final run through. With opening night less than twenty-four hours away, there was too much to do for Peter to give in to what he had convinced himself was a hallucination fueled by sleep deprivation and energy drinks. He had seen the shape in the hall, he knew he had, but he refused to make the thing real, as though thinking of it as anything more than a hallucination would call it back from wherever it hid.

"Like saying the name of Macbeth," he said.

He asked Vince, our King Duncan, to search the theater with him before locking up, not wanting to be surprised by a homeless man looking for a place to nap, and then triple-checked the locks on the front door after Vince left. He propped open the double doors, turned the house lights on, and placed a Paul Simon CD into the theater's sound system. He went back to the office, locked the door, and, certain the sword was by his desk, poured over the list of pre-sold tickets. He gathered up everything he could do at home and shoved it into his messenger bag, leaving him with exactly fifteen minutes worth of work before he could leave the theater. He took deep breaths, partly to stay calm, and partly to check for the scent of dirt and mold.

When he finished, he powered down the computer, threw his bag over one shoulder, and grabbed the sword. He threw the door open, feeling ridiculous with the prop held out like he challenged a knight to a duel.

The shadows beyond his yellow lamp seemed thinner than they had that morning, weaker against the red glow. Grabbing the remote control for the sound system, he didn't kill the CD until he was at the open doors to the lobby, afraid to hear the scratching, scrambling claws racing toward him, confident in his assumption that if he did not give the idea of the thing credence it would not bother him.

It hit him as the music vanished and silence rushed in

that it had needed no thoughts of it to bring it crawling from the dark that morning.

Rather than use the light board backstage, he closed the double doors to the house and flipped the breakers for that section of the theater off. An electric hum that he didn't realize he had been listening to whined down to nothing and vanished. The front door was ten feet from him, the light to the lobby right there at the door, the streetlight outside shining down on the entranceway, illuminating the cracked pavement and oil splattered fast food bags stuffed against the gutter. Cars zoomed by and he felt safe in the arms of the city and her bustling nightlife.

He marched to the door, unlocked it, and flipped the lobby light off.

It had been hiding there, wrapped in illumination like a strait jacket that ripped away with the flipping of that switch, its black shape devouring the light from outside.

It flapped like fabric in the wind, the rustling of linen echoing in the lobby as it reached for him. He fell against the wall, grasping for the light but missing, his fingernails scraping down the switch plate as it came for him. The height of a man on his knees, the mangled shape of sheets twisted in the wash, headless, not the form of a person but moving still like someone racing on hobbled feet, its center whipped like a flag, something like an arm but knotted and brittle grasping for his face. He closed his eyes and turned away as the smell of earth and mold and stale water filled him. It brushed his forehead, the touch like soggy wool rotted to almost nothing pressed against his skin. It was fever warm, thick with illness, and he cried out.

Falling to all fours, desperate to break contact with it, he scrambled to the entrance, his hands slipping on the floor. He shouldered the door and rolled out onto the pavement, was on his feet before he realized he stood, and fought to lock the door behind him.

Through the glass, the lobby was empty.

I realized at some point during the story I had taken my

hand away. Peter gripped it again and took several deep breaths, his jaw trembling.

Then he fell against me and cried.

In ten years, I had seen Peter cry once, at his father's funeral. I held him now until he cried himself out and then held him longer. Words that would make sense of what happened, that would bring comfort or sanity to his ordeal, weren't in my vocabulary. Silent, I brought him a glass of wine and sat with him until sunrise, our eyes glued to the muted television.

Three days later, two shows into the play's run, Peter was rushed to the hospital. I came as soon as Nikki called but it was too late. Cerebral edema, the doctor said. Fluid leaked into his skull and put pressure on his brain. It was quick and painless, they assured me. When pressed for how, they said it was likely genetic and exacerbated by stress.

When asked why, they had nothing to say.

After his funeral, I opted not to renew our lease. Shakespeare's Scottish tragedy had been our final show and, true to its legend, the theater died when it closed.

On the final day of our lease, I came to pack up what was left of our things and put them in storage. I didn't realize it until then, but I hadn't spent more than a few minutes inside since Peter 's death and never alone. There had always been a friend or Nikki or one of the dozens of actors who had performed there while it thrived. I was surprised by how many of them came to pay Peter respects. Many assured me that we had created something special here, that Theatre Obscura had carved out a place in their hearts and would always be with them.

Peter would have liked that.

In the office, the computer gone and posters taken down, I felt his loss more than ever. Throwing his things into a box, I couldn't help but cry. Pictures of us, cast photos, Peter's pen cup painted with our crude logo, all of it stabbed me as hard and painfully as if the Scottish Lord mistook me for Duncan. Peter would never see any of it again, would never write with those pens, would never hang those posters, and that thought made concrete the loss. It's odd how the absence of someone can be a palpable thing, almost tangible in its heaviness, and it pressed down on me then, sought to crush me into the ground.

The leather pouch he had brought back from Scotland sat in the top drawer of the desk.

Gripping it in my hand, it felt warm and fleshy, like a recently removed heart.

"Why did this happen now?" I had asked a day before he died, my leg healed enough to walk on crutches and help at the theater. "We've had this place for so long."

"I don't know," he'd said and shook his head. "I really don't. Let's not talk about it, okay? Not here."

Holding the bag of grave dirt in my hand, I shivered.

I threw it into a box with spools of blank CD's and extra printer cartridges.

It sat in that box through the years since, locked away in a storage container in Van Nuys, until the drinking and the pills became too weak to numb me. Now it's on my desk, in front of my monitor as I type, the air around it alive. Expectant.

I don't know what's going to happen, don't know if it will come for me like it did Peter. But after I write this, I plan to open the bag and pour its contents onto the bed we shared, spread it over the sheets we tangled ourselves in every morning. Wherever Peter is now, all I can think about is following him. It had brushed his forehead and then he died. Peter had never been superstitious, but I am. I never walk under ladders and I never say the name of that play.

"Say it," he teased in the car ride from the airport when he returned.

"No."

"Do it." He tickled my ribs.

I knocked his hand away. "I'm not going to."

"Chicken."

Lying in dirt stolen from a Scottish cemetery, a photograph of us in Rome framed on my nightstand, I'll turn off the lights and this one time whisper into the dark.

"Macbeth," I'll say.

ALMOST

The sheets were cold. She had been curled in them all day, encased in a satin cocoon as autumn storms rolled over the hills and lightning splintered on the bleak horizon. Her hands, lavender blossoms withered in the cold, were twisted in the fabric.

He sat.

Her head rolled toward him as his weight pressed into the mattress.

He ran a hand through her hair and leaned over to look into her face. Her eyes were bloated blood sacs wrapped in soiled gray cloth. Her smile was just as kind.

"Where have you been?"

Rain blew through the open window to pool on the floor beside them. Her voice was the sound of two pieces of silk rubbed together and it rippled across the water. It had fled her corpse with her breath and had waited here, hungry and defiant, ever since.

"Out," he said and kissed her cool dead cheek.

Below their window, someone laughed. The dull rustles of a fading conversation fought the wind and rain. He thought of their first date, their third, their honeymoon. He thought of when she had been warm and radiant.

"I'm sorry," she said. "I didn't want to fight."

"I know."

"This must be horrible for you."

He shrugged.

"I can't imagine," she said, and he almost felt her breath on his neck.

"I need you."

"I know. I need you, too."

It was almost like love. It was enough to bring him back here night after night, to pull him shuffling down winding streets better forgotten and into this house, their house. Into this bed.

Eyes damp, hands quivering, his lips found hers. He lifted her torso into him, her back arching, head tilting to reveal her neck, long and pale and tender, and his lips met the skin there, cool, damp from misting rain, and only her arms hanging limp at her sides reminded him that their time had passed.

He closed his eyes and pressed himself against her. His fingers gripped hers, his head pressed next to her own, her voice in his right ear and in his left and above him and inside of him gasping and fighting for air and begging more, more, don't stop, until he collapsed, sweat soaked and breath starved, and held her.

"Please don't cry," she said.

He almost felt a hand brush the tears away.

"I'm sorry."

She was quiet.

He stared out the window, charcoal clouds cramming the sky, and wondered if he were mad. Not for what was happening, what had been happening since that night when she tried to leave and he grabbed her and they argued and they fought and she raked her nails down his face and he...

And he.

No, he wondered if he were mad for what he was about to do.

"I'm hungry," she said, the word dampened in the air like a flashlight in fog.

"I know," he said.

"Don't tease. You went out. We argued, I know, but you went out for me. I know you did. You always do. Please."

He sniffed. "Give me a minute."

It wasn't long until hot blood speckled her lips and ran over her teeth. It painted her throat and the air around her was alive with movement, vibrations that felt to him like violin strings met with a bow. She moaned in his ear louder than before, so furious in her joy that she didn't acknowledge the source until it was too late.

"No," she said, and he could almost feel her tremble, could almost feel her own tears against his cheek. "Why?"

He pressed his wrist to her mouth, his arm growing weak, his head spinning. "I can't anymore."

In the corner was the last one he had fed her, a drunk divorcee he had picked up at the bar last night. She was wrapped in a plastic tarp and he hadn't yet taken her out to the ocean, taken her to where the others waited beneath the cold dark waves. They'd find the plastic tarp when they found him and maybe they'd understand.

"You can't," she said.

"I'm sorry."

"You're so selfish. You wouldn't let me leave you, and now you're running away."

"Never," he said. "I'll never leave you."

"Never?"

"I need you," he whispered and collapsed next to her, his body growing cold.

It was almost like love.

HIS ONLY COMPANY, THE WALLS

Hi! You've reached Kat's cell. Leave a message.

I think I lost you. My signal's weak out here. I was just calling to say I'm at the hotel and settling in. I bought a bottle of champagne, some French kind I can't pronounce. The girl at the liquor store recommended it. I saw a few nice restaurants on the way up that we could visit, too. We should celebrate. We've been waiting for this for far too long. If I hadn't...

Well, I don't guess that matters now. I've been taking my pills. I hate the things, but I know you want me to take them, so...

Anyway, I'll keep an eye out for you. Try not to be too long. Call me.

Love you.

Hi! You've reached Kat's cell. Leave a message.

Hey. Me again. Where are you? Why aren't you returning my calls? Ummm... just call me back, I guess. I love you.

Hi! You've reached Kat's cell. Leave a message.

Hey. Just checking in, seeing what your status is. About to go out and look for a pharmacy. These things go fast. Want me to pick up anything? Gimme a call. Love you.

Did you call earlier? My battery died and I forgot to put my phone on the charger. It's charged now, so just call back. If you did. Earlier, I mean. Call either way. Please.

Voicemail again, huh? I wish you'd answer. My head's been itching like crazy. It's this horrible feeling inside my skull, like maggots burrowing against the bone and trying to find a way out. I've scratched it until it bleeds, but nothing works.

I'm being gross, aren't I? Sorry. It's just getting to me. This room. The itching. You not calling. I had that dream again, too. Where I came to your work. I shouldn't bring that up, I know. Is that why you aren't calling? I was hoping we'd gotten past that by now. Maybe this was too soon. Maybe I should have canceled this whole trip. What do you think?

I love you.

Walls can talk, you know. Every time someone mutters "If these walls could talk..." they have no idea how close they are to one of the great secrets of the world. Most people have never been able to hear their walls, maybe because their walls have weak voices, or maybe they don't have much to say. But if you spend enough time on the road bouncing around from hotel to hotel, you start to pick up on the subtle whispering that leaks through holes in rotting wallpaper and from behind tacky thrift store paintings of schooners at sea. It's like reading, really. Until you learn how to listen it's just random humming, but once you do you can't turn it off.

I'm wasting away here waiting on you, my only company the walls. It took me a few days to puzzle out their language. I thought it was the hum of electronics or heating vents at first, but then I pressed my ear against the flowery wallpaper and heard your name.

I wish they would shut the hell up. I don't believe a thing they say about you.

This room reminds me of that first weekend we spent away together. Remember? We rented that convertible. Some kind of Chrysler, I think. Seafoam green the brochure said, with Bluetooth and cruise control. The sun blanketed us as we sped up the Pacific Coast Highway, a mountain pressed against your side of the road and the long drop to the crashing surf below on mine. It was raining slightly, and you thought that was strange because of how sunny it was.

"The devil's beating his wife," I said.

You laughed and asked what the hell that meant.

"I don't know," I said. "Just some odd Southern-ism my mom used to say whenever it rained while the sun was shining."

We'd done the typical wine country tour that marked us as tourists, stopping at each winery just long enough to lose a little bit of our inhibitions before heading to the next. A far cry from the stinking flesh and acidic mouths that pressed against us at that punk show where we met.

What was that band called? I can't remember.

The hotel we stayed at that weekend was a lot like this one. The worst room in an otherwise decent place. The wallpaper was the same nicotine stained color and the windows were littered with the same dried out husks of flies that had somehow found their way into the room but never left. What a horrible end for those things, being able to see the outside but not to reach it, pounding their heads against the window until they crushed their pathetic little insect skulls.

Not that any of that mattered to us. We never left the bed.

The couple in the room beside me reminds me of us. They fucked all night last night. I couldn't sleep a wink. Their grunting and moaning blasted through the walls so loud that I could have sworn at one point I was the one fucking. Even the air conditioner, one of those hotel standard issue models with a jet engine crammed inside of it, couldn't drown them out. I cranked the thing up all the way and buried myself inside my blankets, but it couldn't match Mr. and Mrs. Grey next door. Eventually even the walls grew tired of them.

God, I wish you would hurry up and get here. Why aren't you-

BEEP

I miss you. I'm sorry for... everything, you know? Just... just call me back. Please? I love you.

Been staring out the window for so long my eyes have gone weak. I keep thinking I see your car slowing at the traffic light, rainwater cascading from your roof and swirling around your tires. You're there now. I tick off the seconds (135 to be exact) that mark the duration of the red light. All you have to do is turn left when the light changes, pull into the lot and park below my room. 131, 132, 133... It'll change soon and you'll turn left.

The light always changes, and you always drive straight, speeding off into the distance. As the taillights fade, I remind myself that it wasn't really you, just an impostor, some bastard masquerading as you.

The walls whisper amongst themselves, arguing over if it will ever be you. One wall thinks you'll never come, that you'll change your mind at the last minute and decide not to turn. That wall says you'll take the path all the illusions of you have taken. The rest doubt you're coming at all. I tune them out. They're all wrong, aren't they? You'll be here soon.

My itch keeps getting worse, especially at night. I guess

I've been scratching it in my sleep. There are little trails of blood on my pillow when I get up and I can feel fresh scabs hiding under my hair. How do you stop an itch this bad?

The front desk clerk just came by. He wanted to know how long I was extending my stay. I'd originally checked in for four days. I've been here for... God, has it been over a week already? I guess so. Kind of starting to feel like home a little. Well, not quite. Not without you. But close.

I told him "indefinitely" and gave him the MasterCard.

Room service came after that. Cheeseburger, fries, and a coke. I've been racking up quite a tab here. I haven't left the room in the past couple of days in case you call. My cell phone signal is a little weak out here and I'm afraid if I drive down to one of these pitiful neighborhood markets I'd miss you.

I mean, miss your call. I already miss you.

Your phone's probably about to cut me off again. Please just call and let me know what's keeping you and when you'll—

BEEP

Sorry I haven't called in the past few days. The walls were telling me I shouldn't. They said I may be putting too much pressure on you. Am I? I usually don't believe them (they lie so much), but if I am, I'm sorry.

I've lost count of how long I've been here. They bring a credit card slip for me to sign with my lunch every day. I've been sleeping too much. Twelve hours sometimes. It's just so damn hard to wake up, like I'm floating in some warm body of water and to wake means breaking the surface into the icy air above.

You're there also, when I sleep. Just dreams, I know, but still...

I've been doing aerobics. Sounds funny, doesn't it? At least I'm not wearing a leotard. It's just something to occupy my day and stay in shape while I wait. Plus, it's the only daytime TV I can stomach. Have to be in good shape when you come, though, right? I have to be able to keep up.

I've also been catching up on my reading. I've already finished the physical books I brought (*The Stranger* and *Slaughterhouse Five*), and I've moved on to e-books. It's a little hard on the eyes staring at my phone for so long, but it's either that or surfing junk sites.

I almost went for a walk today, but something kept me from it. Part of it was being afraid of missing your call, I guess, but there was something else. It's kind of hard to explain. It was like the idea of going outside scared the shit out of me. I don't know why. Maybe I've been inside these walls for too long. I'm sure that'll change when you get here.

Someone knocked on my door a couple of hours ago. I thought it was you and rushed to answer it, but no one was there. Whoever knocked was fast, I guess. I mean, I instantly opened it. They had knocked damn hard, too, like they desperately needed something. Must have been kids.

Well, I'm gonna go before your voicemail has a chance to cut me off again. Call me, okay? Please? This is killing me.

※ ※ ※

Where are you?

※ ※ ※

Hey. It's me. I just thought of something that tickled the old funny bone. Do you remember that night at your brother's birthday party? When me and your brother got into that fight? Your brother was saying—

Hold on.

...

Sorry. Someone was knocking at the door again. I wish I could catch whoever's doing it. I'd rip the little shit's throat open. What was I saying before that? Fuck. I don't remember.

SHUT UP!

Sorry. Not you. The walls were... Never mind. Never mind the walls. It's best to ignore them.

Are you ignoring me?

Sorry. Forget I said anything. Call me.

Hey. Me again. Of course. How are you? Where are you? You were supposed to be here two weeks ago. I know you couldn't give me an exact date, but this is getting a little ridiculous. I wish you would at least just fucking call me. Why can't you just pick up the goddamn phone and...

Sorry! Sorry. I'm just stressed. I didn't sleep last night. That fucking kid pounded on my door every three or four hours. Of course, he wasn't there by the time I got out of bed. I called the front desk and they said they would investigate. Fat lot of good that will do.

The weather here is awful. It's been raining so much that whatever separates earth from the heavens must have ripped open. The wind rattles the windows so hard I'm surprised they haven't shaken free from their sills. The sky's the color of charcoal when it's turned to ash. Even if I wanted to leave the room I wouldn't in this kind of weather.

I've been watching the hotel across from mine. There's a girl there. A prostitute, I think. Maybe just the local party girl, I don't know. There's always a different guy going in and out over there. In between them she likes to stand against the railing in front of her door and smoke. She's got this stringy blond hair, like she hasn't washed it in days, and she always wears this pink baby doll tee. Her limbs are little more than bone with skin stretched over them and a few bruises painted here and there. She saw me watching her earlier and winked at me. I shut the curtains.

Don't think I'm planning on going over there or

anything. I'm just bored. You know, if you get here before the weather-THAT FUCKING KID'S KNOCKING AGAIN! I'll call you back.

※ ※ ※

Katherine....

※ ※ ※

....

※ ※ ※

...fucking bitch...

※ ※ ※

I'm sorry about that last message. I'm just... you know... I'm sorry. I didn't mean it. I love you. Just please come. I'll make it up to you when you get here.

※ ※ ※

The knocking's gotten worse. I don't know how they get away with it, but they're doing it every couple of hours now. I tried leaving my door open to catch them, but I didn't like that. It didn't feel right, having that door open. I tried asking the walls who it was, but they've grown silent. Thank God for small favors, I guess.

※ ※ ※

I screamed at the kid today, told him I would rip his goddamn tongue out and kick his guts until they were a bloody mush. I guess I went overboard. Someone called the front desk and the manager came to see me. He said that another outburst like that and they'd have to ask me to leave. I can't take that. I've been here for so long now.

What would I even do out there? I have to watch myself.

Guess it's a good thing I telecommute.

At least the kid stopped knocking. The walls have been whispering again, but very softly and only to each other. I can't make out what they're saying anymore. Probably for the best.

I can hear him, shuffling up and down the hall, moving back and forth past my door. He's out there right now. I've been listening to him for the last hour, my head pressed against the door so hard I can see thousands of tiny little stars, an entire galaxy hidden inside my skull. The way his feet sound, it's like he's limping, or maybe pulling one useless foot behind him like a soldier dragging a corpse. Who is he? What the hell does he want?

I keep putting my hand to the knob, thinking I'll swing it open fast enough to catch him. But I can't. I'm worried about who could be out there in that hall. Maybe I'm worried that no one will be there.

The walls only whisper when he's not around. When the shuffling stops, the walls talk amongst themselves. When he comes back, they go mute. I tried asking them why, but they're ignoring me now.

Jesus, I need you here. I need to get out of here, but I just can't. I can't. Not without you.

That hooker keeps watching me. I've got the curtains closed, but whenever I peek out from behind them, she's there, just staring at my window. What's so goddamn interesting about me, huh?

The itching is unbearable. I scratched it hard enough today to pull a little hair out. Maybe there's some kind of lotion or—

Shit! He's outside my door again. I've gotta go. I don't want him to hear me.

He's calling now. I know it's him. For the past three nights, three calls a night. Midnight, two, and four. I called the front desk but talking to them is like talking to the rain.

The first two nights he didn't say anything. I yelled into the phone, but he wouldn't say a word. The last call, the one at four last night, he...

Ah, shit.

He asked about you.

By name.

The voice... Christ, it was strange. Listening to it made my skin feel like insects were crawling all over it, burrowing inside it, laying eggs in it. It was hollow and tinny, but low. Rumbling, like a hearse driving over gravel. It's the voice I imagine tombstones would use if they could speak. And the way he said your name... He drew the syllables out, like he was tasting each one. It came out like "Kaaaaath... rrrrriiiinnnnnne..."

I hung up and took the phone off the hook.

What am I going to do? I can't leave. He's out there in the hall somewhere. If I stay here, he'll come for me, I know he will. I managed to eavesdrop on the walls (they thought I was sleeping) and they said that he would come for me. They sounded frightened.

For the love of God, please hurry. Please.

I'm so hungry. I haven't eaten since... I don't know... I'm afraid if I call room service that when they knock and I answer the door, he'll be there. He's probably there now.

I watched that hooker again today. She had her door open and a pizza box on her bed. She was eating so slowly, grabbing a slice every half an hour or so, raising it to her lips at the speed that leaves change color and chewing with her mouth open. I could smell it, I swear to Christ I could. It had to be a trick of the mind. I mean, there's a pane of glass and a parking lot between us.

She saw me sometime after the third slice. God knows what I look like right now, with bald patches exposing bits of dry, scabbed over scalp. She must have thought I was salivating over her and not the pizza. She put it down and slid the strap of her shirt from one shoulder, revealing a small, pale breast tipped with a brown nipple. She smiled and spread her legs a little, her fingers digging under the waist band and rubbing herself.

I shut the curtain.

The worst part was...

Ah, shit. This is gross.

I... ate... some of the dead flies in the window. The first couple made me gag a little, but after that it was kind of like tofu. Just spongy and flavorless.

I killed her, Kat. Oh my God, I killed her.

The hooker, she was eating cheeseburgers, those little tiny burgers that come in a sack of twenty. She caught me watching her again, smiled, and tilted the bag toward me. I nodded. She stood and walked down the stairs to the parking lot.

I was trying to think of a way for her to get to the bathroom window or wondering if she mashed those burgers down if she could slide them under the door, when she knocked.

"Hey! You the guy been watching me?"

"Yeah. Sorry."

She laughed. "It's okay. Can I come in?"

"I... I can't open the door."

"Is it stuck?"

"No. No, I'm..."

"You're afraid, huh? Like that Howard Hughes guy?"

She couldn't see me, of course, but I nodded.

"Well," she said, "I'm Bree."

"Like the cheese?"

"Yeah, I guess. You hungry?"

"Uh-huh."

"That's what I thought. You looked hungry. I got this bag of burgers here I could share with you, but we got a problem. Can't get them in there without you opening the door."

"Yeah. I've been trying to figure that one out."

She laughed. It was a beautiful sound.

Then I heard the shuffling.

Then a thud.

"Bree?"

There was this wet slap, like raw meat being slammed on a counter.

"Bree!"

My hand hovered over the knob, but I couldn't.

He was there. He came for me. He took her just to get me to open the door. I know he did.

I stood there like that, useless, breathing heavy, crying, smelling those fucking burgers, and listening to this grinding noise like rocks forced into powder on the other side of the door.

Finally, he shuffled off down the hall, dragging her along just like he dragged his useless leg. It sounded like her head bounced off corners as he went.

When I was sure he was gone I cracked the door open just enough to yank the bag through, then slammed it shut and locked it. I slid a dresser up against it and sat on it, eating those delicious burgers from a blood-soaked bag and knowing that I killed her. My stomach was—

BEEP

Goddamn your fucking voicemail! Every fucking time! Fuck!

❊ ❊ ❊

You're not coming, are you?

❊ ❊ ❊

The walls finally spoke to me again. I asked about him, but they refused to say who or what he was, or why he was. Said it would anger him.

They did tell me what he did to Bree. It was so...

They warned me. Told me I had to leave. Said that he had a hard time getting into the rooms, but he would eventually find a way. They said I've been here too long, and he's noticed me because of it. They said he never sleeps. They said I must leave. They begged me not to tell him they talked about him. What is this thing that even the walls fear?

❊ ❊ ❊

He's outside my door. Kat, if you're coming, please hurry. I can hear him breathing against the door. I can see the shadow of his feet through the tiny slit under it. He's been there for hours. I don't know what to do. I thought about calling the police, but what if they think I killed Bree? With my time in the hospital and your police report and everything...

Call me back so I don't feel so alone, okay?

❊ ❊ ❊

He left and that scares me even more. He slid a note under the door before he went. The writing's barely legible, like someone without thumbs who had to grip a pencil in their fist to write. It said: THEY'VE BEEN TALKING ABOUT ME, HAVEN'T THEY?

The walls asked me what it said. I told them. I shouldn't have. They've been hysterical since. One won't stop crying. Another has been praying the whole time. A third one curses me every so often, and the final wall just keeps telling the others to shut up.

Have I lost my mind again?

I managed to fall asleep earlier, but something startled me awake. It was a low moaning, like an animal in pain. I jumped out of bed and turned on the lights. I staggered back when I saw a line of roaches running down the wall. When my eyes adjusted, I could see it wasn't roaches.

I collapsed on the bed. The walls... they were bleeding. That moaning, it was their death rattle. I sat on my bed, powerless, as the life slowly leaked out of them. The carpet soaked it all up like a shag vampire until there was nothing left. The trails of blood left white streaks where it pulled the color from that horrible flowered wallpaper. The streaks look like tears.

Now it's just me.

Kat. I love you so much. I don't know why you never came. I hope nothing happened to you. It's better to think you just stopped loving me, I guess.

It's probably a good thing you never came.

Sorry I'm whispering. I'm in the bathroom. He's in my room. I don't know how. I woke up when I heard the knob turning and rushed in here. He's trashing the room right now, throwing things, smashing furniture. He'll be in here before long. God in Heaven, I hope it's quick. Please, Lord, let it be quick.

Funny that I've finally found God, here at the end. You'll be happy about that.

I love you so much, baby. I'm so sorry I hurt you. I just wish that—

Fuck! He's at the door. Ohshitohfuckohshit! He's—

No!

Hi! You've reached Kat's cell. Leave a message.

...

...

Kaaaaath... rrrrriiiinnnnnne...

PICKED LAST

The playground. That tangle of steel joints and plastic slides was the ultimate crucible as a child, the place where you either shined or were shit. A suburban jungle demanding you claw and scratch for position in a brutal hierarchy of fifth grade politics. It all boiled down to one thing, really: when were you picked?

Picked first and you were king for a day. You were *wanted*.

Picked last and you were despised and ridiculed.

Picked last and you were nothing.

At the age of twelve, this is all you know. You may cry yourself to sleep at night, but you still maintain a grim acceptance of your place, no matter how much it hurts. At twelve, the playground is your reality.

At forty, looking back, you see how it could have been different. How you might have made it different. That guilt solidifies into something cold and raw.

Andy Lumis. He was the kid always picked last. Every school has one. We would line up for kickball or dodge ball, the captains having already declared themselves, and everyone knew Andy would be picked last. You could feel it coming, the team that would be stuck with him sensing it like a doctor with a patient who's not going to make it. The playground was our entire world then and the world did not want Andy.

He knew it, too. How could he not? I saw it in his eyes every time we lined up and he tried to vanish behind the other kids, pushing his glasses up onto the bridge of his nose and fearful, it seemed, that he might not be picked at all.

I was the only one ever glad to see Andy. When you're picked next to last, you're happy there's someone lower than you. Next to last is easier to justify. Maybe it was the luck of the draw. Or maybe you were engulfed by the hulking shadow of the Stookesbury boys and no one saw you until they'd found their teams. It was never because you were rail-thin and wheezed with asthma. Definitely not that. Sometimes I'd catch the glares of my new teammates, or hear the sighs, but I didn't care. I wasn't last and that was all that mattered.

Andy was a target for bullying, a common story for quiet, chubby kids like him. He took his fair share of wedgies and Indian burns and lost a bulk of his lunchtime Jell-O to thieves every year. The occasional fake love letter was even written in his name to Jennifer Vaught, who everyone knew Andy had had a crush on since kindergarten. I'm not proud to admit that I'm the one who started that particular tradition.

He rarely reacted to any of it. I'd watch him sometimes in class, hunched over his pale green desk in the back row wearing a dirty sweatshirt, greasy hair falling over those thick glasses, and I couldn't help but smile. It's not me, I'd think. They could be torturing me. If not for Andy, I would have been the one picked last.

I might have been the one in the woods that day.

I've told myself time and time again that we simply played our roles in the pecking order. I knew my place and it was one notch above him. I had to do it. Even when he was screaming and crying, and blood and shit were everywhere, I had to.

After gym class one day, Todd stole Andy's ball cap. A handful of us were still in the locker room, the smell of old sweat and rusting metal almost covering the musky scent of Coach Logan's Brut spray-on. Coach had left us alone while he repaired a crooked basketball goal and that was when Todd snatched Andy's hat.

"What's this thing?" Todd held the old Cincinnati Reds cap high, examining the white R over the bill as though he'd never heard of the team before.

In East Tennessee, we weren't anywhere near a city with a pro-ball team, but most of the kids were Braves fans all the same. At first, I'd thought that was why Todd grabbed the hat. But I could tell by the cruel joy in his eyes that the real reason was something worse.

Andy tried to grab the hat back, but Todd was taller than him and held it just out of reach.

Jeff Dinkle, who followed Todd around as though he were the boy's assistant, whistled. "That's a 1976 World Series cap. My dad collects those for all the teams."

"I guess it's rare, huh?" Todd asked as he moved around the locker room, keeping the hat away from Andy and shoving the poor kid when he got too close.

"They only made so many," Jeff said. "And that's, what, thirteen years old now? Probably worth a bit of money."

"Man," Todd grinned. "Be a real shame if this got soaked in the toilet." Todd spun away from Andy and headed toward the bathroom.

Andy bounced off a locker as he cut between Todd and the row of stalls. He turned and I was surprised to see how wet his eyes were.

"Give it back," he said.

Todd grinned. "Make me."

Andy's father had been a truck driver. He'd never made much money, barely enough to keep Andy and his mother in their cramped little house with no air conditioning while he was out on the road. A year earlier, he'd been in the middle of his second twenty-hour drive that week and careened off the side of a mountain road. The insurance money kept them afloat, but just barely. Rumor was that Andy's Mom gave handjobs to truckers behind Weigel's Gas for five bucks a pop to keep food on the table. I didn't think it was true then, but who knows? People do what they have to when they're desperate.

Given their situation, Andy never had the Nintendo and Teenage Mutant Ninja Turtles the rest of us did. Andy's house was a few streets over from mine and sometimes I'd see him in the woods, building forts or temples or something with rocks and twigs. They were tiny things, little pyramids of earth and stone. He never played with G.I. Joes in the forest like the rest of us. He didn't even have another kid to share his peculiar imagination with. All Andy had to play with was dirt and rocks. That hat wasn't just the last thing his dad had ever given him, it was probably the only thing.

And so, when Todd said, "Make me," Andy did.

I'd never seen someone move like that. It was so fast, the way Andy exploded. Punch after punch smashed into Todd's nose, blood splattering across the floor and onto the lockers. Todd's head made this dull thud when it hit the ground and the rest of us rushed in to pull Andy off him. He was crying, kicking and screaming, and I knew that if we hadn't grabbed him, he would have killed Todd right then and there.

Instead, he killed him later.

Andy was suspended and Todd came back to school on Monday with a large, white bandage across his nose and a purple splotch surrounding one bloodshot eye. Everyone poked fun at him for getting beaten up. And beaten up by Andy Lumis of all people.

Todd had always traded on his good looks, the nice clothes his parents bought him, and an innate athletic prowess that, even in fifth grade, was something to be in awe of. He'd already had a girlfriend in Stephanie McKnight (God, was she gorgeous!) and, on the surface, seemed one of those people who had been born apart from the rest of us.

Until Andy.

Todd couldn't stand the jokes. Each one pissed him off more and more until finally he kicked Joe Nesbitt in the shin hard enough to leave the boy walking with a limp the rest of the week. After that, Todd sat down at his desk next to mine, gripping the edge of it so hard his knuckles went white.

"I'm going to fucking kill him," he muttered.

I knew he didn't mean Joe Nesbitt.

The way I heard it, Todd's dad used to smack him around a bit. But not in the way that my dad or Steve's dad smacked us around. The rumor was Todd's dad liked to use his belt. Sometimes Todd would show up at the end of the school year wearing a sweatshirt when it was ninety degrees out. Especially the day after report cards were delivered. As I said, on the surface, you'd never suspect any of this. Todd must have learned at an early age how to bury that hurt deep inside of him.

After the fight with Andy, he refused to change clothes with the rest of us in gym class for a couple of weeks. He sat in a bathroom stall until we'd gone out to play basketball, trotting onto the court ten minutes after the rest of us.

I had to run back into the locker room to piss one day and caught Todd in his underwear. Huge red welts streaked down from his ribs before disappearing beneath his underwear. They picked up again on his thigh.

He caught me looking and we both stood there, quiet, neither of us knowing what to say.

Todd finally turned his back to me as he slid a shirt on. "My dad gave me these," he said. "Punishment for letting Andy whip my ass."

I didn't know how to respond. I just nodded, did my business, and ran back out onto the court. Todd didn't come out for a long time.

That Saturday, though, he knocked on my door. Jeff and Steve Myers were with him. They looked like they stepped out of a JC Penney's catalog together: lean builds, close cropped hair (Todd and Steve's blond, Jeff's red), and crisp, clean polos. They made me feel small and wretched in my bargain bin T-shirt.

"Hey," Todd said. "You busy today?"

I shook my head, not sure what they wanted. Todd and I hadn't played together since we were six. That was the year he'd learned the words "shit head" and "loser," after all.

"Stephanie says you told her you've seen Andy playing in the woods before. Is that right?"

I didn't answer.

"C'mon, asswipe." Jeff said it as though it were an affectionate nickname. "We just want to teach him a lesson."

"Why?"

Jeff laughed. "Seriously?"

Todd stared at me, eyes cold.

"Let's go," Steve said. "I told you this cum guzzler wouldn't know shit."

Yes, go, I wanted to say. Get the Hell off my porch with your cowardly three-against-one bullshit. Andy beat you fair and square and you know what? You deserved it, asshole.

I wanted to say all of that. Instead I looked to my feet and shrugged, happy they were leaving.

Steve jumped from the porch. Jeff shook his head, eyes narrow, and spit on my shoe. He hopped down after Steve.

"Come on, Todd," Steve said. "We'll catch Andy when he comes back from suspension."

Todd didn't move. Reaching into his pocket, he pulled out a crumpled bill. "I'll give you ten dollars," he said and held out to me. "Just show us where he plays. Please."

It wasn't the money that made me agree, though ten dollars back then could buy all sorts of toys for a kid my age. No, it was the tremble in Todd's voice. The look in his eyes. He needed me right then. I'd never felt that before and I didn't want to let it go.

We walked through the woods behind my house, a crisp September breeze signaling autumn's approach. The woods smelled wet and earthy that day, even though it hadn't rained in a week. It brought to mind mushrooms and the mold splotches on our basement walls.

"My Dad says these woods are haunted," Jeff said.

"Bullshit." Steve shoved Jeff's shoulder.

Jeff shoved him back. "Fuck you. It's true. I mean, true that he says it, anyway. He says a lot of weird shit after a few beers."

"What's it haunted by then? Dead Indians?"

"I don't know. He says it has something to do with that apartment building over the hill there, the one that serial killer lived in. He says—"

"Shhh." Todd cut his hand through the air and the two of them went quiet.

We followed Todd's gaze down a small rise to where Andy sat, sticks piled to one side of him as he shaped a little mound from dirt and dried leaves.

"What's he doing?" Jeff asked.

None of us answered. We simply watched as Andy patted the mound flat, stacked sticks around the base of it, and then added more dirt. A pyramid began to take shape and, when he had finished piling the sticks up on the outside of it, he turned to gather more dirt and began another.

That was when Todd sprinted down toward him.

Leaves crunched beneath his feet and Andy looked up just in time for Todd's fist to collide with his jaw. Steve and Jeff rushed in to grab Andy, holding him down as Todd kicked him in the face. I heard something crack.

"You want a piece of me now, you fuck?" Todd grabbed a stick from the ground and jabbed Andy in the ribs with it, poked him so hard blood welled up beneath the shirt.

Andy's eyes darted around, unable to focus. He coughed up red spittle and Todd laughed.

"You fucking homo," Todd said. "I've seen you in the locker room watching me change. You don't think I noticed that?"

We all laughed. This was news to us and, to a twelve-year-old boy in East Tennessee, homosexuality was far funnier than it should have been.

"You don't think I remember what happened on the playground last year?" Todd was screaming now, and I looked around to make sure no one's parents were coming.

We were alone.

"You don't think I remember that?" Todd kicked him again and the rest of us stared at one another. What was he talking about?

"You fucking homo," he repeated. "What do you want me to do now, stick my dick in your ass?"

Andy cried and coughed, blood and snot all over his face.

"Please," Andy begged, his voice so tiny.

"You hear him? That *is* what he wants." Todd grabbed Andy's pants and yanked them down to his ankles.

"Todd," I said, my voice shaking with panic. "He's learned his lesson, man. Can we just—"

Todd flicked open his pocketknife and pointed it at me. "Shut up."

I looked to Steve and Jeff, but they stared at the ground, still holding Andy down by the shoulders. Todd's disciples.

Todd took his knife and cut Andy's shorts off. Andy wailed. Jeff and Steve squirmed. I couldn't move. I didn't know what to do, didn't know what Todd was going to do.

"Todd, I think he's had enough." It was all I could manage, and it came out so quiet I don't know if he heard me.

Steve nodded and muttered something.

Todd ignored us. He was focused on Andy as he paced around him, breath coming in short, quick bursts. He stared at the crying, quivering mess his friends held down for so long that I thought it was over. I thought his rage had died and that we could all go home.

Then he shoved the stick inside Andy.

I've never heard someone scream like that. It was so loud, so high-pitched, that I thought my eardrums would burst. The pain and violation and loss of dignity and innocence that erupted from Andy's throat hit me hard and has stayed with me all these years. Whenever a child cries or a dog yelps or even the whistle that comes when I turn up the hot water in the shower, it's Andy's screaming I hear.

Tears poured from Andy's eyes like a water hose, blood and snot mingling into pink slime on the side of his face.

I had to look away as Todd went to work. Blood and shit were everywhere. Jeff (or maybe Steve?) clamped his hand over Andy's mouth to quiet the screams, but that was worse. It changed the sound into a squeal like a pig being slaughtered. He thrashed around, dirt and crumbled leaves dusting the air, but Jeff and Steve, whose faces had gone white and eyes hollow and both looked like they would soon vomit, refused to let him go.

Why aren't they stopping this, I thought. Why isn't anyone stopping this?

Why am I not stopping this?

But I couldn't. I couldn't do anything. That was my place in the pecking order: beneath Todd and above Andy. Again, I thought: that could be me, and, God help me, I was thankful for what happened *to Andy*.

Todd finally threw the stick to the side. "Is that what you wanted? Or do you want more?"

Andy pressed his face into the dirt, weeping and trembling. He had given up, his screams little more than soft nonsense now pulsing into the earth.

Todd unzipped his pants and pulled his pecker out. I was surprised to see it stood tall. All that sickness, that butchery, it turned him on.

He stepped over Andy's body and straddled his back. He spit into his hand and started rubbing himself.

"Is this what you wanted?"

It was too much for me. My stomach heaved and I turned to the side, my lunch spilling onto the ground.

Todd laughed at me. Tears streaked his face, too, as though he knew the irrevocable horror he dealt to the boy under him but had gone too far to turn back.

The paralysis that had gripped me finally broke. I scrambled up the rise and ran. Crashing through the woods, my legs pumped as fast as I could will them. Tiny branches smacked against my arms, clawed at my face, but I ignored them. I had to get away. I had to get home.

Sticks crunched and feet pounded the earth behind me. Something heavy slammed into my back and I hit the ground, face first, my chin scraping across a small rock, my lip busting open on a fallen branch. My mouth filled with the taste of hot copper.

"You tell anyone about this," Todd whispered in my ear, "you'll be next."

His breath on my neck was hot and wet and I knew that he meant it. I knew he meant it because I could feel his erection grinding into my thigh. I knew he meant it because I knew he secretly *wanted* me to tell, he wanted a reason to do that sick shit he just did to Andy to me.

Andy was on his feet now, crying, and moaning. He struggled to pull his pants up as he limped away. Jeff and Steve stood there, neither willing to give chase. Even Todd seemed to have lost the taste for it all. He only watched as Andy disappeared into the woods.

His grip loosened and I sprinted the opposite direction of Andy. I kept expecting to hear Todd behind me again, but no one came after me. I made it home and shut myself in my room. Pressing my face into a pillow, I cried. I cried and cried and cried, and then dropped to my knees and prayed to a God who had surely turned His face away from those woods that He could forgive me for what I just did.

I prayed He could forgive me for what I didn't do.

I never talked about it. No one did. I pretended I had the flu and stayed home from school the next week. It wasn't until I came back that I found out about Andy.

The human digestive system is a delicate thing. Different kinds of food, things like corn chips or hard candy, can sometimes scratch you on the way down. It's no wonder four ounces of crushed glass mixed with a two-liter of Sprite caused so much internal bleeding.

"What would cause someone to do something like that?"

everyone asked. "Why would anyone feel they deserved to suffer so much?"

I knew.

I didn't go to his funeral. Brooke Walton told me Todd did, but I don't know that I believe that.

Summer came and I forgot all about Andy and what we had done in the woods. Or, at least, I told myself I had. I drew my monsters and played my video games and pretended Andy had never existed. I pretended Todd had never done those things and that I had never been too much of a coward to stop him.

It wasn't until the next fall that any of us saw Andy again.

School had started and I avoided Todd and his cronies like the plague. We didn't have any classes together and I refused to go onto the playground. I knew that, with Andy gone, I would have been next. I would have been the one getting beaten up behind the slide or having my lunch stolen. Worse than all of that, I'd now be the one picked last.

Rather than suffer that embarrassment, I spent recesses in the library. I did my homework and read C.S. Lewis. I tried to draw my monsters, but most of them ended up looking like Todd or Andy and so I gave up drawing altogether.

Then one day, walking home from school, I took a shortcut through the woods. The air was cool, the autumn sun casting the forest in red and gold, and every step I took crunched leaves beneath my feet. Yet something did not feel right about the woods that day. I didn't feel like someone watched me or that there was any kind of presence. Rather, I felt alone. Isolated. It was as though I was the only living thing in the forest. I had never felt like that in my own neighborhood.

When I climbed a hill and saw the little pile of sticks and stones, some strange little pyramid that had been sculpted in those woods, I ran.

My bladder emptied when I heard something crashing through the woods behind me.

Busting through the front door, I hurried to my room. I shut and locked the door, closed the blinds, and pulled out my Bible. I read something about Ezekiel that I couldn't understand over and over again.

I started reading it out loud when the scratching at my window began.

There was no rest that night, no sleep for a guilty kid afraid of what might be trying to get into his room. I was so tired and scared the next morning that I didn't even need to pretend I was sick. Mom was suspicious, but she let me stay home from school all the same. By mid-morning I had convinced myself the noises and the pyramid were simply my guilt getting to me, but I still didn't think I could face school. It was a Friday, anyway, so why not a three-day weekend? I could relax, I told myself. Catch up on some reading, finish a few Nintendo games—it would be great.

But it wasn't great. That entire weekend was filled with nightmares. I don't remember what they were, not exactly, but every time my head hit the pillow, I found myself in the woods or on the playground.

At school Monday, everyone was abuzz with the news: Jeff had been kidnapped. Someone had broken the window to his bedroom and snatched him right out of bed. The police had no leads and the search parties his parents coordinated had turned up nothing.

It wasn't until Todd cornered me in the bathroom that I put two and two together.

"Hey, dink," he said as he threw me into one of the stalls. He came in after me and shut the door. "Have you seen him?"

I shook my head. "No."

He grabbed me by the collar. "Don't lie to me."

"I'm not! I haven't seen Jeff since last week!"

"I'm not talking about Jeff." Todd's voice cracked as he spoke. "Have you told anyone about what we did?"

"You mean what *you* did."

Todd didn't say anything for a long while. Then he

opened the door to the stall and moved aside.

I inched my way past him and started toward the bathroom door.

"Jeff made one of those things last week," Todd said. "Those little stick houses. I caught him in his backyard with it."

I just nodded. I didn't know what else to do.

"I made one too," he said, and I ran from the bathroom.

A month went by before Steve disappeared. He had taken the trash out and never came back in. Steve's brother said that thirteen or fourteen little "dirt forts" were found in Steve's room. Apparently, he had been bringing in rocks and dirt for weeks.

Two weeks later I woke to someone knocking on my window. I looked up, expecting to see Andy's pale, dead face staring down at me.

It was Todd. I opened the window and he climbed in.

"You have to help me. He's after me."

"I know," I said. "He caught me in the woods one day."

His eyes went wide. "You saw him?"

"No, but I know it was him. I saw his pyramids."

He started to cry. "He was in my bedroom. He was watching me sleep—I don't know for how long. I woke up and there he was. He was naked and didn't have on his glasses and there was this scar on his chest and... What are we going to do?"

"Do you want to stay here tonight?"

He nodded and I was glad. I was scared, too. More scared than I had been that day in the woods, even. We turned on the Nintendo and played *Contra* until we both passed out in the floor.

A loud thump startled me awake. I sat up, rubbing my eyes as I scanned the room.

Todd was gone. The window was open, a cold breeze blowing my drapes around. I jumped up and was about to close it when I saw him not thirty feet from the house. He stumbled toward the woods.

I wanted to yell, but he disappeared into the trees. Slipping my shoes on, I hopped down from the window. The early morning quiet was surreal, the air frigid and everything with this strange dark-blue tint to it. I guessed it was only five o'clock or so.

I had the thought I should let Todd go. For all the things he'd done, he deserved whatever waited for him deep within those woods.

But I knew that if Todd disappeared, I would be the last one left.

I would be the only one.

I ran after him. He was hard to keep track of once I got into the woods. The trees blocked what little light there was. I stumbled aimlessly for several minutes before his white T-shirt caught my eye.

"Todd! Wait!"

I jumped over a little mound of dirt (a pyramid?), landing in a puddle. I bent over to see how much mud I had gotten on my pajamas and, when I looked up, someone stood in front of me.

I stumbled back, almost screaming as my eyes adjusted to the darkness.

"Jeff?"

It *was* Jeff. And there was Steve, standing off to Jeff's side.

"Shit, are you guys okay? Everyone's been worried about you."

They blinked in unison and turned their backs to me.

"Have you guys seen Todd? I was—"

The words caught in my throat as I stepped past them.

Todd knelt on all fours, a pale, thin figure standing over him. Naked, it caressed his cheek. Shadows covered the face, but I knew who it was.

Once again, I ran through those woods, fear twisting my gut, adrenaline filling my veins. This time, though, no one followed. They didn't need to. They knew where to find me.

I climbed back into my room and slammed the window shut. I ripped the mattress from my bed and put it in front of the window, sliding the dresser against it. Then I grabbed my Bible and prayed.

When Mom came into my room, I was hysterical. I couldn't answer any questions. They tried to move the dresser away from the window and I tackled my father to keep it in place. It wasn't until a neighbor called the police because of the noise that they were able to get me out of my room.

In my garden, now, all these years later, I think of Andy. As a parent, I feel a deep sadness for what happened to him. That such evil can be forced onto children keeps me up at night worried about my own.

And maybe that's why this has all come back to me now. Maybe becoming a father is what triggered it. I had almost convinced myself none of it had ever happened and then...

My parents put me into an institution for the rest of the year it had happened and all the next. They thought I had lost my mind, that I had narrowly escaped the kidnapper that had taken Todd, Steve, and Jeff and my fragile brain couldn't deal with it all. They were much closer to the truth than they realized.

The police questioned me a dozen times over the next several years, but what the hell could I tell them? Better that my mental issues blocked all memory of the event. I faked that for so long that it became real. I stopped dreaming of Andy, stopped wondering what had happened to Todd and his friends. I made a "miraculous recovery," as the doctors said, even if I wouldn't piece my memory back together.

My parents moved us across the state before I was even released from the institution. I was so happy to hear I'd never again see that neighborhood. I'd never again fear what walked through those woods.

In my new school, I reinvented myself. I juggled both athletics and academics with an ease I never thought possible. Captain of the track team, I went on to be the valedictorian of my graduating class. After college, I got married and started my own marketing firm.

My wife recently gave birth to a beautiful baby girl. When she laughs, I can't help but melt. She's made a perfect life somehow better.

And then a week ago I was here in my garden. I pushed and pulled dirt and rocks around, trying to shape it for a row of tomatoes I still haven't planted. I screamed when I saw the two little pyramids I'd crafted from earth and stone. I screamed and the memories came rushing back.

I wasn't safe. I had never been safe. Andy had just waited, biding his time to torment me with my worst childhood fear. When I saw him at my window last night, pale and thin faced, I knew.

He hadn't forgotten about me.

He had picked me last.

CHASING THE REAPER

The fire alarm was screaming by the time the El Camino's engine cranked. Thick banners of flame flickered from the door of our motel room, long columns of angry smoke curling out through them like a nest of vipers.

In the distance, sirens wailed.

"C'mon," I said. It was taking too long. I'd have to peel out soon whether I saw Virgil or not.

Blue and red lights danced against the tree line less than a mile away.

Bewildered heads poked from their doors. They looked like Whac-A-Moles. I wished I had time to bash them all back into their holes.

My watch alarm began its usual plinky requiem, a digital funeral dirge for freaks like us. I shifted to "Drive."

A dark shape shot from the room, flames reaching for its backside.

The news reports would later comment on the fire, on the occult imagery in the room that seemed to be the ignition point, and on how it matched similar incidences in hotels across the Southeast. But most of the eyewitness reports would focus on the naked man that seemed to leap from the mouth of Hell itself, stopping long enough to bow and flip the dazed vacationers the bird before sliding into the El Camino.

When we were safely on the interstate, Virgil grabbed my wrist and looked at my watch. "Shit, Worm. Think you could cut it a little closer next time?"

"We shouldn't have gone so far from the hotel."

He shook his head. "We done been over this a hundred

times, man. Keeps them guessing. We don't want them connecting my blowing up or your eating a shotgun shell to that shit at the hotels, do ya?"

"Whatever. It was my turn anyway."

He grabbed a pair of jeans from the floorboard and struggled to slide them on. "Was it? Shit, man. I don't remember. Once I'm in the zone, I'm in the zone."

"Of course it was my turn."

Virgil scratched his chin. "Didn't you just go through that mulcher?"

"Yeah, but you drove that motorcycle into the side of a Wal-Mart *and* ate that Japanese blowfish. That means I was supposed to do two in a row. Well, shit. Three now."

He chewed his fingertip. "Huh," he said.

"Well?"

"Well, what?"

"What was it like?" This was our favorite part. A play by play of what each death had been like. We'd never used explosives before, and I needed to know.

He lit a cigarette and stared out the window. A giant puff. An exhale. Then he laughed. "Damn. It's hard to describe."

"Well, you better."

"Okay. It was like cumming."

"What?"

"Listen. You know how when you get with a fine piece of ass, and she knows she's fine, and she spends all night teasing you? And you get this pressure just building up to the point where you can't think straight. And then-BAM! You blow. And it's this sweet agony as all that pressure pours out of you. That's what it's like, only times a thousand."

"So, it didn't hurt?"

He smacked the back of my head and cackled like a madman. "Course it fucking hurt. I blew my goddamn guts out. Shit, man. What's wrong with you?"

"Tell me about the hurt."

I should have been the one telling this. That bomb was meant for me.

"Alright." He smiled. "Alright. Well, first Time does its trick." This was our way of saying that once the adrenaline starts pumping and the senses become hyper-aware, everything around you seems to slow to a crawl. It's the fight or flight mechanism, honed through a million years of evolution to get folks out of the situations that Virgil and I put ourselves into. "Then you feel a small spark right here—" he tapped his belly "—where the bomb is strapped. That spark gets hotter and hotter until it feels like knives stabbing into you, hot knives twisting and tearing. Then those knives turn into a bunch of saw blades, cutting you up and getting bits of you tangled up in them before they rip their way out and shoot off in every direction."

It was quiet for a long time.

"What?"

I shook my head. "Nothing. Just wish I could have felt it, is all."

"You'll get your chance."

I wasn't so sure.

The ritual could only be performed on the night of a new moon. For whatever bizarre occult reason, this meant we could only come back once a month. The ritual also had to be completed before midnight and within six hours of dying, or we were just so much useless meat come 12:01am. And, of course, one of us had to be in the shape to perform it. This had never been much of an issue. Two of us, we each go every other time.

Problem was, Virgil had become a junkie.

Let me tell you how it starts. A little taste of death, literally. A night of binge drinking, tequila laced with mercury, PBR injected with anthrax, and God only knows what else. Add to that enough cocaine to burn out an elephant's heart and it still surprises me he lasted the four and a half hours he did.

His body had been intact, so it wasn't long until he

jumped back up and wanted to do it again. But the next month was my turn. I cranked it up a notch (shotgun to the face) and, when I returned, Virgil was antsy. Anxious. Already talking about taking a meat cleaver to his privates.

Shoot-outs with cops, razor wire nooses, knife fights in alleys, gang beatings, chainsaws, bear wrestling, an industrial strength hose of Clorox threaded up the rectum —you name it, we've done it. And every ounce of abuse we served ourselves was exquisite. If you've never died and came back (and I'm assuming you have not), it's the best high in the world. Coke, heroin, sex—nothing comes close. It's like copping a feel from the eternal. So, while I could understand Virgil's addiction, I had my own monkey to feed.

And this ape was starving.

"How many paid the toll?" This was Virgil's way of asking how many he had sacrificed for the ritual.

"Too many," I said.

The ritual didn't require the death of anyone else, but Virgil had convinced himself that whatever gods or spirits brought us back demanded sacrifice in return. I refused to do it when it was my turn, but for Virgil it had become a good luck charm. On those nights I'd almost worked up the nerve to sneak off and put as much asphalt between me and Virgil as I could, it was the memory of their faces that prompted it. The unneeded sacrificed.

Needless to say, I'd never worked up enough nerve.

Virgil sighed. "Just tell me how many."

"The girl behind the counter, the mall security guard... um..."

"Don't forget that old bag I shot before I blew," he said.

"Yeah. So, three."

He shook his head. "A bomb should have killed more than just me and three others."

I was glad it didn't. "Well, shit, man. You jumped the gun. If you had waited for people to show up..."

"Yeah, yeah."

But he hadn't waited. He couldn't have. How can a junkie wait even one minute for a fix?

We decided on Birmingham for my run. We made it there the day of the new moon, stopping at a few small towns in Mississippi along the way to raise some cash. That mockery of a car barely rattled off I-65 and down University Avenue to a shitty motel with a dried-out pool. It was named, with that flair for genius that only rundown motel owners can muster, "Motel."

The Saudi behind the counter tried to force us into two rooms, but Virgil told him how we had just driven down from Massachusetts and wanted to celebrate our honeymoon. He still charged us forty bucks for the night.

We spent the day walking around campus, bumming cigarettes from students and trying to pick up chicks.

"You alright?" Virgil kept asking me.

"Yeah," I'd say. "Just excited is all."

But the truth is I was nervous. When the time came, I knew, I just *knew*, that Virgil would weasel me out of it. That was what he did.

When I was fifteen, Virgil knocked on my window one night. When I opened it, he'd grinned ear to ear.

"How much money you got saved up?"

"I dunno. Fifty bucks?"

"Perfect."

He told me he knew a party we could go to and that he was going to help me pop my cherry. Virgil was two years older than I was and, for some reason, had taken me under his wing when we moved into the trailer park. At least, that's how he always referred to our friendship.

"This chick, Janine, she's got tits for days. For *days*," he'd said. "You buy her pot and she'll screw your brains out."

We went by his dealer's place, this fat son-of-a-bitch named Lester who was half-Vietnamese but always wore a cowboy hat and listened to rap music. Virgil said we needed a lot because you can't walk into a party empty handed and so I handed over the whole fifty, my week's pay for mowing yards.

The party turned out to be me, Virgil, and Janine at her trailer. Her Dad was hauling a load up to Louisville and she had the place to herself. She was attractive. Maybe not by Hollywood standards, but to a shy fifteen-year-old in East Tennessee she was beautiful.

And she liked me. That was the kicker. No girl had ever liked me before. But we both loved *Alien* and Coen Brothers movies and spent the night making each other laugh.

When it came time for Virgil to pull out the bag, he smiled and asked if it was all right. Janine's eyes lit up and she said it was, long as he shared.

"Well, you got to do something for me first."

"What?"

Virgil motioned her into the back bedroom. She followed.

The door closed.

My palms were covered in sweat and my foot couldn't stop tapping on the floor. I kept waiting for him to open the door and say, "I told her. She's really into you. Go get her."

He never did.

I fell asleep on the couch watching Andy Griffith reruns. He woke me close to dawn and drove me home.

"What happened?"

He laughed. "I'm sorry, man, but when I got her back there, she was all over me. I couldn't help it."

In all those years, he had never once mentioned my fifty dollars.

We stopped at a Birmingham favorite, some greasy spoon called "Al's," and ordered a couple of burgers and some ranch fries. Two girls sat next to us, college girls, their spring sundresses the color of wildflowers and their laughs infectious. Virgil and I pulled our table closer and started talking.

He was all over the black girl. They joked and touched each other's arms and compared tattoos.

The blonde didn't seem as interested in me.

"What's your name?" I asked.

"Christy."

"Your friends call you Chris?"

"My friends do, yeah."

We made idle chit chat, where you from, what are you studying, that kind of thing.

It wasn't difficult for me to talk about her classes. I was much smarter than I typically let on. Virgil didn't care much for "book smarts." He thought it was the mark of a pansy. It had been so long since I used that part of my brain, it took a moment to dust it off.

Christy's eyes were twin pieces of jade and her voice carried the soft sound of hidden music. Even though she didn't care for me, I fell for her right then and there.

Virgil and Lisa kept giggling as he cracked jokes at the expense of a morbidly obese man behind them. The guy was five hundred pounds if he was fifty. He had a laptop out and made a show of writing, hitting the keys hard and cocking his eyebrow as though he were processing incredibly deep thoughts. Every now and then he would let out a sigh, pause, and then force a "Eureka" expression on his face before going back to work.

"Hey," Virgil yelled. "What are you typing over there?"

"I'm a writer," the man said.

"Well, no shit. I kinda figured that, the way you're making sure we all looked."

He blinked. "It's a screenplay."

"No shit?"

Virgil scooted his chair over close to the guy, reading over his shoulder as he critiqued the script. Lisa pulled over next to them and kept giggling. It was easy to see the big guy was embarrassed. He had come out for a little attention, a little acknowledgement that he had something special to offer. He didn't expect Virgil.

"Your friend's an asshole," Christy said.

"Lady, you don't even *know*."

She swung her bag over her shoulder and stood. "I should go. Lisa! You coming?"

Lisa waved her off. She sighed.

"You have class?" I asked.

She scowled. "Yeah. Calculus. Blek."

"Mind if I walk with you?"

She shrugged.

I told Virgil I'd be back in a few but he was too busy telling the big guy how cliché his inciting incident was.

"What's your story?" she asked as we walked down a narrow street lined with old houses.

"What do you mean?"

"I mean that you're not from here, are you?"

"How'd you know?"

"I have a sixth sense."

"We just kinda been driving around."

"You mean Virgil's been driving around."

"Huh?"

"You've been following him."

"I wouldn't say that."

She laughed. "Of course you wouldn't. You're the lap-dog. Lapdog's aren't allowed to say things like that. They aren't even allowed to think them."

I stopped. I don't know what shocked me more: that the stuck-up bitch had said it or that it was true.

She kept walking but I didn't follow. I knew her kind. She was beautiful enough to get by with casual cruelty and was probably so used to hurting people that she didn't even realize she did it. To her, she was only being honest.

It was hours later before I got back to the hotel room. Virgil sat on the bed watching "Antiques Roadshow."

"Where the hell you been?" he asked.

"Just walking."

"Uh-huh. You get any?"

"No."

"Me either. Cock tease." He flipped off the television and sat up. "So, I planned out the night."

"Yeah?"

"Lisa was telling me about where her parents live, this rich, stuck up neighborhood. *Mountain Brook.* It's the kind of place where nobody ever had to work for a living."

"We don't work for a living."

"The hell we don't. Work harder than some fucking investment banker. Anyway, she gave me their address."

"Why would she do that?"

"She's having a birthday dinner there tonight. Can you believe that shit?"

"And she invited you?"

"Yeah. I think she just wants to freak out Mommy and Daddy."

"So, what's the plan?"

"Well, when dinner's almost finished, I'll hop up on the table." He pulled his pistol out. "And put one in your forehead. When they're all screaming and everything, I'll do the rest of them."

I swallowed. "Sounds boring," I said, hoping to dissuade him from killing anyone else.

"No, man. Here's where it gets fun. We'll take all our ingredients with us. I'll shoot them all in the gut and, while they bleed out, we'll make them watch you rise. One last 'fuck you' to the rich before they die."

I had to hand it to him. It was definitely ballsy. Mass murder in a neighborhood like that, performing the ritual at the exact same spot he killed me, all of that could get us busted.

Talk about a rush.

"I don't know about everyone else."

He punched me in the chest. "Get over that shit," he said. "I'm gonna fucking murder you, my man. Bang bang. Execution style."

Would he? When the time came to chase the Reaper, would he shoot me or turn the thing on himself?

That night we arrived on time. We'd stopped at the mall and bought some new clothes, trying our best to look all Abercrombie & Bitch for the evening, and sauntered up the walk to a house that probably cost what my Dad made in his entire life. I kept trying to work out how to convince Virgil not to kill anyone else, but I'll be honest: If it required others to die to get my fix, I wasn't entirely sure I'd say no. That's a horrible thought, I know, but it's also an addict's thought. And I was, if nothing else, a junkie.

Virgil rang the bell. I half expected a butler to answer.

Lisa opened the door, smile wide, hair done up and a black cocktail dress hugging her curves.

"Happy birthday," Virgil said and kissed her cheek.

She pointed to the cooler in his arms. "What's in there?"

"Your present," he said.

She looked surprised to see me but muttered a thanks for the bottle of wine I gave her. Virgil had told me you had to bring wine to a dinner party.

Lisa led us into a small parlor, red and gold furniture sitting on dark wooden floors.

Christy stretched out on one of the sofas. She smiled and raised a glass.

I sat across from her.

Lisa took Virgil's hand. "Let me show you around."

When they were gone, Christy stared at me. "I didn't expect to see you tonight."

"Virgil told me... Invited me, I mean."

"Ah. Is that so?"

"It wasn't like that."

"It's okay." She drummed her fingers on the glass and looked around the room.

We were quiet for a long while.

"Lisa's parents here?" I asked.

"No."

"I thought it was a birthday dinner."

"It is. Her parents are out of town, so we decided to have dinner. When she met Virgil, I guess she found her present." Christy laughed. "I make her sound like a slut."

It was my turn to look around the room.

"So, Worm. What kind of name is that, anyway?"

"Nickname. I've had it since I was a kid."

"Virgil give it to you?"

I didn't answer that.

She adjusted her dress. "What do you do?"

"What do I do?"

"Yeah. You're not a student."

"How can you be sure?"

She tapped her temple. "Sixth sense. Remember?"

"Right."

"Well?"

What the hell? "We kill and rob people."

She blinked.

"We hightail it from town to town, get our fix, steal what we need, and then move on."

"You kill and rob people."

"Well. I've never killed anyone. Virgil does that. I don't care much for it, truth be told. But the stealing's alright. I'm pretty good at it, actually."

She grinned, thinking it was all a joke. In a way, I guess it was.

"What's your fix?"

"You'll never believe me," I said.

"Try me."

"Dying."

"Dying?"

"Yeah." I noticed we had both leaned forward, scooted closer toward one another on our seats. "When we were in New Orleans a while back, we met this guy claimed to be a bokor. You know what that is?"

"Some kind of voodoo thing, right? Like a priest?"

"No. Not really. *Voudun* is a religion. Bokors are... well. They're into some mean and nasty shit. Way this dude explained it to us was that what he does and voudun came out of the same place in Haiti and share a few

140

things, but they're about as similar as Methodists and Devil Worshippers.

"Anyway, Virgil had bought some smack off this guy and it turned out to be laced. He had the shits for a week. So, we track the guy down and Virgil's gonna do him, ya know. Right there in the guy's house. Right in front of his kids and everything.

"This guy's begging to live and I'm begging Virgil to leave, and the kids are crying and that's when the guy says, 'You let me go and I'll show you how to chase the Reaper.'"

"Chase the Reaper?"

"Yeah. That's what he calls it. So, Virgil's fucking with the guy and says, 'Sure. Why not?' The guy sets up all this stuff—it's so gross I won't even go into it—and tells us what to do. Then he asks Virgil to shoot him.

"Bam! Just like that, Virgil blew his brains out. No hesitation. I freak out, start grabbing up shit and trying to get out the door, but Virgil stops me. He wants to go through with the crazy ritual."

"And...?"

"And it worked."

She leaned in. Her smell was vanilla and strawberries.

"The guy came back. No shit. Just hopped right back up like it was nothing. We tried it the next month and got hooked."

"Show me."

"Huh?"

"Show me."

She brushed a hand against my knee.

I didn't know what to say.

A gunshot went off upstairs.

"Shit," I said.

Christy jumped up, eyes wide, hands trembling. "What was that?"

"Fucking Virgil," I said and grabbed her hand. "That asshole."

We ran up the stairs.

Lisa was on the bed, naked, blood leaking from a wound in her abdomen and spilling over the comforter. She was pale and her breath shallow. Christy screamed and ran to her.

Virgil fired again.

Christy fell against the wall and slid to the floor. It took a moment for the blood to start pouring. She looked down at the wound, eyes filled with confusion.

"Goddammit, Virgil! This wasn't the plan."

He stood naked, a cigarette dangling from his mouth, the gun smoking in one hand. "Shit, man. Weren't no dinner party. She just brought me here to fuck with me. Goddamned cock tease."

If we did the ritual real quick like, maybe there would still be time to call 911 and get the girls some help. "So, I guess we'll do it right here," I said.

He grinned that wild grin of his.

I reached for the pistol. "You son-of-a-bitch, don't you even think about—"

He aimed the barrel at his crotch and fired.

The smell of cordite hung in the air. My ears felt like they were stuffed with cotton.

Virgil rolled around on the floor, screaming in pain and laughing like a wild man as his blood soaked into the carpet.

Lisa gasped. She had lost so much blood. She squirmed some, but she'd be gone soon.

Christy, too. She stared at Virgil, her head cocked to one side. She opened her mouth to speak but coughed and blood dribbled down her chin instead.

I kicked Virgil in the ass. He screamed.

"You prick! It was my turn! MINE!"

He laughed. When he spoke, his voice was slurred and scratched. "C'mon, Worm. I had to. That bitch needed to know, man. She needed to know I can't be beat. I'm invincible."

Naked, holding his mutilated crotch, blood firing out

from an artery between his legs in long arcing spurts, he didn't look invincible to me.

I grabbed the cooler and went to work setting up for the ritual. It was only ten thirty. There was plenty of time.

I caught Christy's eyes.

"Don't."

She kept staring, blood dribbling from her mouth.

"I want to do this. Okay? I do. This is my choice."

Virgil coughed. "What are you talking about?"

"Her," I said. "She thinks I just do whatever you tell me to do. She thinks I'm your lapdog. That's what she called me. *Lapdog*. Can you believe it?"

He laughed and rolled onto his back. He'd gone white and the spurts firing from his crotch had grown weaker. "You are, Worm."

"What?"

"You always been my bitch." He laughed even harder. "My lapdog... That's good."

A high-pitched whistle came from his throat. His head flopped to one side and he was gone.

The tears stung my eyes.

When I finished setting up, I grabbed Virgil's bloody ankles and tugged. His head flopped again, and dead eyes stared at me, bored into me, that stupid grin still plastered on his face.

I moved around to grab him by the shoulders. When I did, I caught sight of Christy. Even dying, she was beautiful.

She looked at me, disgust painted on her face, and shook her head.

Virgil thumped onto the floor.

To Hell with him.

I stomped over and fought Christy's rings from her fingers. She kept staring at me, never blinking, never looking away.

Her lips were soft and much hotter than I thought they would be when I kissed her. They tasted of blood and vanilla lip balm.

I tangled my fingers in her hair. "Let's get one thing straight up front."

She wheezed, the life almost gone from her, as I ripped away a handful of the hair I'd need.

"Next time is my turn," I said.

I put the gun under her jaw and fired.

TABULA RASA

The attic floor creaked above him. Gabe sat on their bed and stared out the window, twirling the ring on his finger round and round. Outside, a young couple walked by holding hands and laughing.

Inside, a moan drifted through the house.

The rhythm of the creaking floorboards above grew faster, almost frenzied. Gabe couldn't listen anymore. He clutched his cane and struggled down to the first floor. He turned the television on, letting an infomercial for eHarmony drown everything else out.

It had started early today. He had rolled over before the alarm went off to find the bed empty, the sheets still warm from where Tomas had been sleeping.

Gabe put a pot of coffee on and thought of how they used to take each other in the mornings.

Footsteps pounded down the stairs and the television clicked off. Tomas entered the kitchen wearing only his boxers. His golden skin glistened with sweat.

"Good morning," he said and moved to kiss Gabe on the cheek.

Gabe placed a hand on his chest. "Not before you shower. Please."

Tomas nodded. "Yeah. Sorry." The red light blinked on the coffee machine and he poured them both a cup. "I'll take a quick one," he said, sipping from his cup as he left the kitchen.

Gabe normally loved the way his husband smelled, how the thick musk of him lingered under accents of lavender. But after he had been in the attic, the scent was wrong. It was sour. He was filthy and ruined and Gabe didn't want that touching him.

His cell buzzed on the counter. It was Jeremy. He answered.

"Hey, Dad."

"Hey, Jeremy. Early morning for you, isn't it?"

"Yeah. New site going up. Trying to get a head start on the scaffolding." Engines rumbled in the background, muffled voices muttering incoherently around them. "How you doing?"

"Great," he lied. "Fantastic."

"Good." A pause.

"Jeremy?"

"I just wanted to wish you happy birthday."

"You and Ashley should bring the kids down. Nothing like summer in the Keys."

"Yeah. Maybe."

"I miss you guys."

"We'll see. Mom hasn't been feeling well. I don't feel comfortable taking off until she's up and around."

"What's wrong?"

His son sighed.

Gabe expected a *What do you care*. He wouldn't have blamed Jeremy for it. Instead his son was silent and that hurt even worse.

"Is she okay?"

"She's fine, Dad. Just tired. She's breaking her back working."

Gabe didn't know what to say. She'd only worked part time when they were married. Between that and the alimony he hadn't considered she might be hurting for cash. He wanted to dig deeper but knew Jeremy wouldn't open up. It was a miracle his son called at all. The accident had been a double-edged sword that way.

"I gotta go, Dad."

"Love you."

The line went dead.

"Who was that?" Tomas wore a flannel bathrobe, his dark hair wet and messed. He kissed Gabe on the cheek and hugged him from behind. The smell of soap and lavender hovered around them and Gabe could almost forget what Tomas had been doing all morning.

"Jeremy." Gabe sat the phone down.

"You okay?"

"Yeah. Of course."

"Wanna walk and grab some breakfast?"

"Sure."

"I'll get dressed." Tomas kissed his cheek again and rushed upstairs.

It wasn't until he was gone that Gabe realized his husband hadn't mentioned his birthday.

Mornings in Key West were slow affairs. The entire island took hours to stretch and yawn and pull itself awake. Before noon most of the people encountered were tourists, couples on their honeymoon or the elderly trying to remember younger days. All of them shot wary glances at Gabe and Tomas as they walked arm in arm down the street.

When they had first began seeing each other, Gabe had assumed the glances were because they were gay. These days his paranoia ran a different route and he imagined that every couple they passed whispered to one another as to why a young, beautiful man like Tomas would be walking around with someone twenty years older and crippled.

They stopped at the tiny outdoor café where they had spent their first evening together. Gabe waited for Tomas to mention it, to tell him this was the start of a romantic birthday celebration, but he never did. They ate their food and chatted about reality television while stray roosters begged for scraps at their feet.

That first night together (had it been three years already?), sitting in almost this exact spot and listening to reggae music sprinkle from tiny speakers on c-stands,

Gabe had scattered breadcrumbs on the ground and a fluttering of tiny wings surrounded their table.

"You're a sweet man, Gabriel." Tomas' blue eyes had held him and, for the first time in his life, Gabe had wanted to kiss another man.

Now his husband treated him with almost the same detachment as he regarded the roosters. The passion they used to share, once a palpable thing, had thinned to a few gossamer strands that still wound around Gabe but seemed to barely brush against his husband.

Tomas shifted gears to politics as he watched camera-toting tourists gather around the tacky signpost announcing the southernmost tip of the United States. Gabe had the feeling that Tomas wasn't talking to him; he was simply talking.

"Do you love me?"

Tomas looked his way and blinked. "What?"

"Do you love me?"

"Of course I love you." He grinned. "Don't be ridiculous."

After breakfast they made their way down the street, the humidity sticking Gabe's shirt collar to his neck. This was the route they had taken that first night, drunk, leaning against one another to keep from stumbling.

They had met at one of the many bars claiming to be Hemingway's original hangout. Gabe had been in the Keys for a real estate seminar. He was counting the dollar bills stapled to the walls when one of his fellow seminar-goers challenged a group of young guys to a tequila-drinking contest. The two groups slammed shots around the trunk of the giant tree growing through the building's center. Eventually everyone trickled off except for Gabe and Tomas.

After leaving the café they had walked through the ancient streets of Key West, shrouded by tropical growth and buffeted with the sounds of a never-ending party that seemed two blocks away at all times. Tomas had told him the island's stories while showing him the sights; an old pirate well rumored to still hold treasure at the bottom, the antebellum house where James Audubon painted his birds, and the home that once held Robert the Haunted Doll.

He explained that the name Key West was a corruption of Cayo Hueso, the Isle of Bones. "When the Spanish landed, all they found were bones. Bones everywhere. In the trees, scattered across the ground, stacked against rocks. One tribe of natives had slaughtered another here and left them to rot."

"Why?"

Tomas had shrugged. "Who knows? The Spanish spread rumors of curses and something they called 'clay demons.'" A laugh. "Silly stuff, I know. I used to be a tour guide. We always talked about how the clay was a metaphor for the way myths and legends could be shaped to fit each new culture. But at night here, after all the drunks pass out, it's easy to mistake the wind in the alleys for whispering."

"You must have been one hell of a tour guide."

They shared an electric smile.

Gabe had fought the temptation to put his arm around the young man. He'd known Tomas was gay after hearing him mention an ex-boyfriend, but Gabe was not. He had been married for twenty-seven years and had two grown children. He had thought about men at times, but not until Tomas had the desire gripped him so strongly.

They passed the funeral home where Dr. Karl Von Costle had kept the body of Elena del Hoyos for seven years. He remembered how Tomas had grabbed his hand for the first time that night while standing in front of it, telling how the doctor had loved her so much that he had stolen her body from its tomb and brought it home, coating it in wax and replacing pieces with the softest velvet. She hadn't loved him in life, but in death he molded her into the Elena he dreamed of, an Elena that would never leave him. It was a disturbing tale, but Tomas had managed to find the beauty in it.

Now they walked by without a word.

At home, Gabe poured a glass of juice and sat on the back porch. A breeze blew in, heavy with the smell of the sea. He leaned back, the rough wicker chair groaning beneath him, and examined the chipped paint overhead. The porch's ceiling, like most in Key West, was painted sky blue, an old sailor's tradition to keep evil spirits away.

He wished it worked.

"Are you going to sit here for a while?"

"Yeah," Gabe said. "I'll probably read some."

"Okay."

Tomas went inside and pounded up the stairs. The attic door opened and closed.

Gabe fought not to cry.

The accident had changed everything.

They had been married for less than six months. Gabe had moved into the bed and breakfast Tomas managed a few weeks before the ceremony. It was supposed to have been the start of a new life.

Then Margot's breakdown came. He loved his now ex-wife and hated what his midlife coming-out had done to her. But how could he live a lie? It wasn't fair to her or him. He had driven north to Orlando, desperate to visit her in the hospital. His children refused to let him into the room. The things they said still kept him up at night.

Distraught, he'd sped home, down interstate 595 through the Everglades, a storm battering the SUV. Vicious winds threatened to blow it from the road and Gabe's knuckles had gone white gripping the wheel. As the storm intensified, he crept along and planned to take the next exit to wait out the rain.

That's when the little blue hatchback pulled out in front of him.

The brake hit the floor, but the SUV kept barreling on. Gabe cut the wheel to the right, tires grasping at the ground and slipping, the world spinning around him, white streaks of rain swirling into the windows. He tipped, wet concrete rushing up to his window, the bag in the passenger seat crashing into his shoulder.

Black.

Tomas was with him when he awoke in the hospital. A dozen broken bones wrapped him in pain. His hip had been shattered and, though eventually rebuilt, the nerve damage kept him from being able to live life to its fullest. He had to reinvent himself, learning how to walk again and how to define a relationship without physical intimacy. He was told that as he adjusted to the pain medication he may one day regain sexual function, but every month spent unable to make love to his husband sapped whatever hope he had in that regard.

It was determined the brakes had been faulty, a factory defect that had gone unnoticed. The settlement was enough to buy the bed and breakfast, closing it off to the public and converting it into their home. Those renovations were some of Gabe's happiest memories, the newlyweds joined together in painting and filling their new house with antique furniture. The settlement ensured neither of them would ever worry about money again.

They soon had bigger things to worry about.

Gabe woke to a scream.

Covered in sweat and shadow, he struggled to remember where he was. He glanced at the clock on the nightstand. It was after three in the morning.

The screaming echoed through the house, high pitched and watery.

It was that goddamned thing in the attic. Tomas had sneaked out of bed and gone up there. Whatever they did, it enjoyed itself.

Another scream shot through the place and the windows rattled.

He fought his way from bed and hobbled over to the bathroom, not even bothering to grab his cane. Splashing cold water onto his face, he caught sight of the ruined lines of surgery after surgery peeking above the waistband of his pajamas. A bottle of prescription sleeping pills sat on a shelf in the medicine cabinet and he shook one out. He downed it with a palm of water and paused, examining the bottle. How easy to swallow them all, to lie down and never get up again.

Tomas stepped into the bedroom a few minutes later, a streetlight cutting through the window and igniting red scratches on his chest. They locked eyes.

"I... I'm sorry we woke you," Tomas said and crawled into bed.

"Are you?"

A sigh. In the dark, the blankets rustled.

"Tomas?"

"What?"

"Listen. I was thinking we should take a trip. Maybe go to New Orleans. There's a blues festival."

"I don't like the blues."

"You used to."

More rustling. "No," he yawned. "*You* like blues music. I only tolerated it."

Tomas was asleep in less than a minute, the sweat sprinkling his flesh carrying that sour scent. Gabe watched him drift off, grabbing his cane and gripping it until his hand went numb.

The ceiling creaked above him.

He stepped into the hall. The shadows were thick on the staircase. The door at the top wasn't visible and he was afraid Tomas had left it open. Yet, as his eyes adjusted, he could make out the shape of the deadbolts fastened along it and holding it closed.

Curiosity nagged at him and he struggled up the steps. At the top he pressed his hand to the wood of the door, imagining he could feel his husband's lust threaded into the grain.

It shuffled around on the other side.

How many times had he stood here, fantasizing about murder? But he was afraid of going into the attic, afraid of facing his sins and finding out what the repercussions might be for stopping what he had set in motion.

A pathetic moan leaked into the hall from behind the door. It reminded him of the sound Margot used to make when he had worked her up enough to almost beg for him.

Gabe's hand went to the locks. For a moment he thought he felt warmth blossom in his groin, a stirring he hadn't felt since the accident. He shrugged it off as a trick of the sleeping pills taking hold and made his way down the stairs.

It scratched at the door behind him.

Tomas began cheating on him mere months after the accident. He'd turned a blind eye to it at first, knowing his husband had a need that Gabe could no longer fill. When Tomas came to him one day and told him he was in love with another man, Gabe's heart broke.

"It's not that I don't love you," Tomas had said, tears in his eyes. "I'm just confused, you know?"

"Are you leaving me?"

"I don't know. I don't want to leave you, but..."

He had trailed off, eyes fixed on his lap. Gabe had wanted to punch him, to feel his jaw shatter. But, more than that, he wanted to grab him, to pull him close and make love to him.

And he couldn't.

He knew who Tomas had been seeing. A sculptor who made his living as a tour guide, a young man with sandy hair and piercing eyes.

Kyle.

Kyle ran ghost tours in the evening, ending in an alley behind one of the bars on Duval Street. His last tour ended after midnight. It always finished with a ridiculous story about how the land behind the alley was cursed, how when the Spanish came and found bones stacked three feet high that the ones found in this small area were too gnarled and deformed to be considered human.

Gabe tracked Kyle there a few nights later. They argued, Kyle telling him he was an inadequate old man who needed to let go and get on with his life.

The cane had hit the tour guide's skull with a sound like thunder echoing from the walls of the alley. Kyle crumpled to the stones, blood gushing from a wound in his face.

Gabe hadn't meant to strike him. He sure as hell hadn't meant to split his face open. Frightened and horrified, he knelt over Kyle and checked the tour guide's pulse.

"Please, God," he'd whispered, searching for the rhythm of Kyle's heartbeat on his throat, "let him be okay."

Tears streaked Gabe's face.

"I didn't want any of this."

Kyle's blood flowed through the cracks in the cobblestone.

"I just want Tomas, want him to be happy at home again. That's all. Please."

Something shuffled through the alley behind him.

The setting sun glowed in the trees. Gabe watched it through the kitchen window, remembering how he and his husband used to be awed by escape artists and fire-breathers during the evening celebrations at Mallory Square. He wondered if they could make it to the coast tonight before everything ended as he stirred sauce on the stove. Gabe had made carbonara for his husband on the first night of their honeymoon and hoped that the recipe held some kind of magic to rekindle their fire for one another.

Tomas had been in the attic most of the day. More and more of his time was spent behind that locked door and Gabe worried what went on in there. The sounds of sex filled the hallway several times a day but other times,

times like now, there was only silence. That bothered him even more.

He took a pan from the stove and removed the bacon. He poured the grease into an empty peanut butter jar and crumbled the red strips over the pasta.

"Tomas!"

No answer.

"Tomas! Dinner's ready!"

Silence.

Goddammit, he could at least have the decency to eat with Gabe.

He grabbed his cane and fought his way to the attic door. He raised his hand to knock but stopped.

The soft rustle of whispering leaked through the cracks.

Ear to the door, he recognized his husband's voice. The speech wasn't discernible. But the hushed tones, the lilt in his words, told Gabe all he needed to know.

Downstairs, he ate dinner by himself, not bothering to steady his shaking hands.

※ ※ ※

The night was quiet. Gabe sat in the dark kitchen, shadows draping him, and watched the acorn shape of a cotton seed bug climb the outside of the window screen.

A creak. The attic door opened and closed. Stairs groaned as Tomas shuffled down. He passed through the kitchen as quiet as a ghost and opened the fridge. White light spilled across the linoleum.

"I made carbonara."

Tomas jumped, his hand going to his chest. "Gabe? What are you doing sitting in the dark?"

"You've been up there all day. I figured you had to eat some time."

"Sorry. Time slips away from me in there." He pulled a Tupperware dish from the fridge and walked it to the microwave. As he passed the table, Gabe caught a whiff of the thing's musk. It made his stomach convulse.

"What have you been doing in there all day, Tomas?"

His husband shut the microwave door and pressed a series of buttons. It hummed to life.

"You know what I do in there," he said. He walked back to the fridge and grabbed a bottle of water.

"You haven't been doing that all day."

Tomas shrugged. He unscrewed the cap on the bottle. Took a large drink. Wiped his mouth with his forearm. "We just..."

"Just what?"

"Just held each other."

"Christ."

"What? This is what you wanted, isn't it?"

Gabe stood. "What are you talking about?"

"Never mind."

He wanted to go to his husband, to hold him, to make all of this go away. But the four feet across the kitchen might as well have been miles.

"Tomas, let's leave here."

The hum of the microwave filled the kitchen.

"Get out of Key West," Gabe went on. "Go someplace where we don't have to deal with hurricane warnings and hundred-degree heat. We can sell this place."

"This is our home."

"Yeah, but we could buy a house anywhere. Or maybe we don't. Maybe we just travel. See the world. You always wanted to travel."

"Stop doing that."

"Doing what?"

"Making up what I want. You always do that. I never wanted to travel, I never liked the music you think I do. I don't even like Italian food, for fuck's sake. You have never known who the hell I am."

"Don't say that. I love you."

"No. You don't, Gabe. You love this... this *idea* of me that you came up with. You created the man you wanted way before your accident. The only problem is that I'm not him."

A headache threatened to split Gabe's skull open. He took a deep breath and tried to stay calm.

Tomas chuckled and wiped a tear away. "He told me, Gabriel. He told me what you asked for."

The microwave dinged.

"What?"

"He came here for a reason," Tomas said, thrusting his finger toward the ceiling. "And you damn well know it."

Gabe shook his head. "It can't talk," he said, refusing to personify the thing in their attic the way Tomas had.

"He can."

"It never has before." Aside from that first night in the alley, it had never done more than moan and shriek.

"Maybe not. Maybe he was waiting, I don't know. But he told me what happened in that alley." He pulled the Tupperware from the microwave.

Gabe's blood went cold. "Nothing happened."

Tomas hurled the dish across the room. It slammed into the wall, white sauce splattering, Tupperware bouncing from the floor. "Stop lying to me!"

His stomach felt empty, hollow, like his life had been ripped away through his abdomen and was never coming back.

"He's changed, Gabe."

"Changed how?"

"Go. See for yourself."

They held each other's gaze. Tomas' eyes, so beautiful in the wan light leaking through the window, were cold and unforgiving.

Gabe nodded. He grabbed his cane and hobbled up the stairs.

At the top, he fumbled with the deadbolts. The knob was hot and damp in his palm. Tomas's sweat, no doubt. Gabe twisted it and opened the door.

The smell of the thing crashed into him. He wondered why musk was the dominant smell, why the thing never seemed to eat or piss or shit. The boards creaked under him as he stepped into the room and the stale scent of old sex drifted up from the floor.

A candle burned in the corner. A mattress sat beside it, soiled yellow and speckled with dark stains. The thing lay with its back to the door, its shadow twitching, distended ribs rising and falling with each breath. Across its misshapen back a dozen orifices glistened and pulsed, a body formed solely for sex.

Its head twisted around to peek over one shoulder.

Warmth flooded Gabe and he was shocked to feel an erection straining against his pajamas for the first time since the accident.

The thing smiled and he wanted to go to it, to feel it pressed against him, to taste each of those throbbing slits.

He took a step closer and gasped at its piercing eyes and sandy hair.

It stretched onto its back, gnarled joints creaking as fingers too long to be human rubbed over pale gray flesh. Eyelids draped down, head straining back on an impossibly thin neck, a moan bubbling up its throat.

Gabe stumbled through the door. Slammed it behind him. Slid the locks into place.

Its face, the hair, the eyes... There was no mistaking it. It didn't just look like Kyle anymore.

It was becoming him.

"Please, God. Please."

He couldn't find a pulse on Kyle's throat.

Something shuffled through the alley behind him. He yelped, spun, fell hard on his ass.

"Please," someone mimicked from the dark. "God. Please."

Cold fingers gripped him as he recognized his own voice. Had someone recorded the entire incident?

"I just want Tomas to be happy at home again. Please." The recording grew louder, pounding in his ears as shadows dripped along the walls.

The dark pressed closer, pulling tight around Kyle's body.

"I just want Tomas to be happy at home again. Please."

"Stop it," he said.

Kyle's blood pooled under him, filling the cracks between stones and vanishing into the earth.

"I just want Tomas to be happy at home again. Please."

"Stop it!" Gabe clutched his cane to his chest.

The shadows wrapped around Kyle's body.

Something moaned.

It scratched across the cobblestones on all fours. Pale gray skin ripped away from the shadows gripping the corpse, clambering on top of the body like a palsied crab. Its face featureless, its flesh a sickly blank white. Malformed bones popped and cracked. It sat on Kyle's chest, the empty face cocked to one side as though it examined Gabe with eyes that did not exist.

Gabe's heart threatened to erupt from his chest.

Pale hands raised into the air on crooked arms, the head tipping forward. The gesture was surprisingly human.

Well?

He understood. It was insane, he knew, but God help him he understood.

"Do it," he said.

A long finger, skin like old paper stretched over it, tapped against Kyle's forehead.

A ripple rolled over the flesh on the thing's skull. Features pressed into the skin from behind, the vague outline of a face.

"Tomas," the shadows mimicked.

The blank flesh scurried back into the dark, a wave of shadow crashing over Kyle's body and obscuring it from view.

Gabe fought to his feet and hurried from the alley. He rushed home and waited for the police to come and drag him off to an asylum, where they would hold him for murder and talk of clay demons.

They never did.

When Tomas made inquiries, the authorities told him Kyle had been emailing with an ex-boyfriend in Miami and probably drove there to see him.

Devastated, he found comfort in Gabe's arms.

"I'm sorry, Gabriel. I should have never let myself get attached to someone else."

Gabe held him and kissed his cheeks and wondered if his prayers had been answered.

Weeks later, after dreaming of the fleshy *thing* in the alley most nights, Gabe heard the scratching in the attic. He knew it had come for him.

He had rolled over to warn Tomas to stay in bed, but his husband was already gone.

Knife in hand, Gabe had gone looking for him. He found his husband holding the thing around the waist, thrusting into it, its head buried in the pillow, Tomas' face pure bliss. Tomas later explained it had drawn him in without reason, like it gave off a pheromone that was impossible to ignore.

"This will work," he'd told Gabe after calming him. "I'll never have to go looking for someone again. We can stay together, and no one will ever get between us."

"We'll stay together," Gabe had said and pressed his head against Tomas's chest. "Forever."

His husband's arms wrapped around him and he knew what had happened in that alley, knew deep in his gut what transaction had occurred. He had made a sacrifice and the demon had come to answer it.

"It's not Kyle."

"Not yet," Tomas said. He ran a hand through his dark hair and leaned against the sink. "But it doesn't matter."

"What do you mean, it doesn't matter?"

"I love him."

The words hit him with the same force his cane had

smashed into Kyle's face. Gabe dropped into a chair. "What...?"

"I love him." He wiped a hand down his face and sighed. "It sounds crazy, I know, but I can't help it. He doesn't just look like Kyle, he *feels* like him, the way he touches me, the way he looks at me." He took a deep breath. "I don't blame you for what you did to him. I drove you to it and... Well, without that I'd never have what I do now. But you and I, we can't go on." He wiped a tear away. "I can't live a lie."

The hollowness in Gabe's stomach spread, threading through his veins and dissolving him from within. He flexed and unflexed his fingers, struggled for breath.

"I'm sorry, Gabe. I really am." Tomas walked by him and back up the stairs.

The attic door closed.

The world ripped apart at the seams. Nothing could ever be beautiful again, he knew that, felt it in his sinking stomach as he sat in the dark in an empty kitchen and stared at his wedding band. He had recreated himself for Tomas, had ruined Margot and ensured he would never have a relationship with his children again. He had bought this place for his husband, had given himself completely to him, and now he was being tossed aside.

He had lost Tomas for good this time, the finality of it aching in his bones. Even now, he knew his husband cuddled against that thing infesting their attic. He imagined Tomas whispering to it, brushing sandy hair from its face and kissing it the way they had once kissed, telling it he loved it in the same sweet voice he had told Gabriel on their wedding night. Hot flesh pressing together, taking it inside of him...

Gabe shot to his feet. He had to move, had to do something. He grabbed his cane and thought he would go for a walk but instead found himself climbing the stairs.

"Kyle" saw him first. Gripping Tomas' back as he thrust into it, it locked eyes with Gabriel. It was the same look the real Kyle had given him in the alley that night.

He gripped his cane so tightly his hand went numb.

Tomas turned toward him, eyes filled with something like pity. Pity for an old, useless man who had been foolish enough to think his husband loved him. Pity for the broken man spying on a carnal act he could no longer take part in. No longer love, just pity.

Fire flooded through him, clouded his thoughts. Tears rolled down his cheeks, dripped from his jaw and crashed to the floor. He wanted the fire to burst free from his skin, to consume the house, to climb the walls and reach into the attic and burn the lovers to ash on their filthy mattress.

Tomas must have seen the change on Gabe's face and he screamed.

Gabe brought the cane down, cutting the scream off, and then again, over and over, the smell of blood in the air covering the musk in the room.

Rolling the bodies into a tarp and dragging them down to the Land Rover had been an ordeal. Hefting them into the back dug fingers of agony into his hip and he'd ground his teeth against the pain, telling himself it would be worth it in the end.

In the alley, the dark again came. It reached up at the scent of blood and seemed to sniff the air like a thousand writhing serpents. He gave his offerings and made his prayers, leaving after a quivering lump of featureless flesh pulled the bodies into the shadows.

That had been three weeks ago. He'd slept on the blood-soaked mattress every night since, waiting. Sleep never came easily. Tomas's bloody face waited for him every time he slipped into the dark. He woke crying every morning, afraid he had been wrong, afraid he had killed his husband for nothing. The story of the Isle of Bones came back to him and he knew that those creatures with flesh as malleable as clay were the reason the natives had been slaughtered in the first place. That's why they didn't eat or shit or piss. They fed on pain, didn't they?

The agony in his hip was almost unbearable. His prescription for pain medication had run out three days earlier and he never bothered to renew it. He hoped the side effects might vanish without the chemicals in his system. He took deep breaths and thought of the first night he'd ever spent with Tomas.

As he leaned back into the mildewed pillow, he almost smelled the lavender scent of his husband crashing over him, could almost feel his warm skin and pouty lips, could almost smell the sour musk that had been absent since the thing was disposed of.

Fingers ran down his torso and his pants grew tight. He strained against them, anticipating the lips that met his ribs. Opening his eyes, he grabbed Tomas' skull and held it close, tangling his fingers in dry, withered hair.

His husband's face was mangled, skin sagging along the cheeks and ears missing. The eyes were two deep, empty holes of red pulp, bloody meat that glistened in the candlelight like the pulsing slits covering his twisted body.

Gabe closed his eyes and moaned as Tomas took him into what might have been a mouth. He clutched at gray flesh in desperate ecstasy and wondered how long he would have to wait to see his husband's blue eyes once more.

HESTER COHEN

She had deep throated a shotgun on the stairs. That was the crux of things, wasn't it? He wanted to look at the stopped clock on the wall, at the dripping faucet in the bathroom behind him, at a crack running along the ceiling. Yet her body sagged against the wall not six feet from him, loose clumps of flesh spreading out on the staircase. The inside of her skull was a Rorschach stain behind her. Blood from her neck pooled beneath her, soaking into her dress and crawling down the stairs toward the floor.

Irwin sat on the top step, his body painted in cold sweat, and tried again to look at anything but her. There was a painting of the Tuscan countryside above her, some generic green and yellow piece bought at discount from a department store. Beyond her were windows clouded with dust and blurring the yard into splashes of green.

Their cell phones sat charging on a table by the front door.

She kept his attention. Even in death she kept him focused on her.

He should call the police.

Hester's insides leaked out onto laminated wood in front of him.

He should definitely call the police.

But there she was, between him and the phones, blocking him like she had always done.

"Fuck you."

The hum of the AC vibrated the air.

"Do you hear me?"

A car honked next door.

"I said fuck you, Hester."

A large bit of bone fell and clicked against the stair. It tumbled down the steps, a gory Slinky leaving a sloppy trail almost to the floor.

"FUCK. YOU."

The tears rolled hot from his chin and stained his sweatshirt.

He needed to call the police.

"Is this what it comes to? Huh?"

He sucked in a sharp breath and the smell of gunpowder tickled his nostrils.

"Do you hate me this much?"

He knew she did. All the nagging, the insulting, all of that had been a precursor to this moment. She yelled at him daily. Told him he wasn't a man. Ridiculed his paunch and fading hairline. She laughed at the charcoal angels he scrawled on canvass in his office at night. She wished aloud that the cancer had taken him rather than cowering into remission.

Yes, she hated him that much. He believed it. He would have believed even if she hadn't thrown a coffee mug at his face this morning, missing him by an inch to shatter against the wall, Hester ranting about all the dick she'd tasted at her company in the past year, all the different ways her coworkers had penetrated her, then laughed at him for crying.

"Cuck," she called him. "Beta piece of shit." She asked if his vagina was hurting. Asked if had any balls left at all. She wanted him to yell, to scream, to push her, to hit her, to display some kind of aggression.

He didn't. He simply wept at what had become of them.

He needed to call the police.

Irwin grasped the rail and pulled himself up. His legs and back were tight and refused to unravel. A few steps down and past her body was his phone. Call the goddamned police and let them haul her away and be done with it.

He took a step. The floor was colder here. His shoes were in his closet. Should he go back and get them? He did not want to step barefoot in her blood.

She had wanted that, though. That was why she had done this here. That was why she had taken the phones downstairs and plugged them into the chargers. She had planned it so he would have to walk over her, *through* her, to make that call.

She had burned his charcoals last night. The alcohol helped, he was sure, but whiskey couldn't make you do what wasn't already in you. The hate was there. The drink brought it out, yeah, but it was there. Why had she hated him so much?

"Don't mistake my kindness for weakness," he'd said once, repeating some meme he had seen online.

He wished he had never said it. She snorted and replied, "You shouldn't mistake your weakness for kindness."

Irwin turned and went back to his room. Slipped on his shoes. Took several deep breaths.

His neighbors liked to sit on the porch on nice days like this and watch their kids play in the yard. He could open the window and yell for someone to call 911.

No. She would win that way too.

Irwin stomped back to the stairs.

"Hester Cohen, I want you to listen to me. I am going to call the police. I'm going to call the police and I'm going to do it myself and there is nothing you can do to stop me. You hear?"

Her hand flopped from her lap and onto the stair.

He nodded. Okay, then. Time to do this.

The first step was simple. The second groaned under his weight. He gripped the rail so hard his knuckles ached.

The third step.

Fourth.

At the fifth he froze.

Light sparkled from the gold anklet he had bought her for their third anniversary. She had loved him then, before the doctors, before the "episodes," before the pills. She had been heavy then, not as heavy as now, but still a large girl. He had found her beautiful, called her "plump" and kissed every inch of her at night. That was before the extreme diets. Before the vomiting. Before she hated how she looked in a dark way he knew had nothing to do with her appearance.

"Fat fucking cow," he said and instantly regretted it.

The tears came again, crashed over him and swept him away. He fell onto his ass, the impact vibrating up his spine and into his skull. His bladder thumped against his pelvis.

"That was cruel. I didn't mean it, Hester. I love the way..."

He trailed off when his eyes drifted to where her face had once been.

"I have to piss."

He went back upstairs and to the bathroom. As he went, he thought of all the names she called him in the beginning, "handsome" and "sweetheart" and "stud." He thought, too, of the names she had called him these last two years, "pussy" and "queer" and "limp-dick."

He fell to his knees, clutched the toilet, and emptied his stomach inside.

When he went back to the stairs, she seemed smaller. Her body had shifted, a red trail glistening down the wall in a strange arc.

"Do you know," he said, "how hard this is going to be to clean up?"

He slumped down onto the top stair again.

"I mean, think about it, Hester. First, they gotta get your body outta here. Then they gotta clean up all the little bits and pieces. Something will have to be done to the wall. Clorox, maybe. Definitely paint over it after."

The gun sat next to her. It was the length of her leg. How had she managed to do it, to put that thing in her mouth and still pull the trigger?

"I need to call the police," he said.

Somewhere a dog barked.

He wiped his eyes with the backs of his hands.

"I hate you. You hear me, Hester? I fucking hate you."

The silver wedding band slipped from his finger with no resistance. He held it up and peered through it, examined Hester's body through a circle that once represented fidelity. Love. Trust.

No matter how he twisted the ring, he couldn't fit her inside it.

He flung it at her. It bounced from her breasts and rattled down the steps, the echo of its spin climbing from somewhere below.

Irwin had been the one to notice the signs. They weren't hard to see. First came the diets. Low-fat. No fat. Atkins. Keto. Paleo and vegan. Weight watchers. Even goddamned fruitarianism. She starved herself for days and then binged on pizza and ice cream, only to break down sobbing and force herself to vomit. He asked her why she tortured herself like that, why she would put herself through so much pain to change something he found beautiful about her.

"Of course you wouldn't understand," she said.

She gave up on the dieting after a year and things grew worse. She stayed up all night and slept all day on the weekends. She'd take random sick days off and not leave the bed, refusing to let him watch over her. Her evening drink turned into three, four, and then soon she was going through two or three bottles a week. Some days she would close all the curtains and play the sound of rain when it was a gorgeous eighty degrees and sunny out. She'd lock herself in the bathroom for hours at a time, doing God knows what in there.

He convinced her to see a doctor. They gave her pills. They setup appointments with a therapist. But then she stopped taking the pills.

"They make me dull," she'd said.

Then she stopped seeing the therapist.

"I don't like the way the asshole looks at me," she'd said.

One night shortly after that, Irwin decided to make her favorite meal. Pappardelle with a homemade Bolognese. The sauce alone took almost six hours to cook. He had spilled some on the tablecloth when he spooned it into her bowl, a tiny bit of grease staining the fabric.

Hester beat him with a rolled-up magazine for that. Beat him like he was a goddamned dog. And he had taken it. He had known she was hurting somehow and hadn't wanted to make things worse and so he stood there and took it.

She had never looked at him the same after that.

He needed to call the police.

Irwin stood and stretched, the muscles in his back still fighting to untangle.

His doorbell rang.

He froze, unsure what to do. Had someone heard the gunshot? How long ago had it been? It felt like he had sat on these steps for hours, but that couldn't be right. And surely a neighbor would have heard that shotgun firing, that loud thunderclap muffled only by his wife's face?

The bell rang again.

His stomach twisted. Acid rose in the back of his throat. Was the door unlocked?

"Come in," he said.

The doorknob jiggled.

Clicked.

The door creaked open.

A small boy stood in the doorway. He couldn't have been older than eight, dark hair falling to his eyes, a boxer holding a victory stance on his shirt.

"Mr. Cohen? We were playing ball and heard—"

He saw Hester and the color drained from his face.

"It's okay, son," Irwin said "What's your name?"

The boy stood still, one hand on the knob. A croaking sound leaked from between his lips.

"What's your name?"

"Is she..."

"Yeah."

The boy swallowed.

"Listen. I need you to do me a favor. See that phone there?"

He turned to look at it, his hand never leaving the door.

"I need you to grab it and toss it to me. You think you can do that?"

The boy took a step back.

"No! Please. Listen. Just grab that phone and throw it to me. Then you can get outta here. Okay?"

He looked up at Irwin.

"Please?"

He nodded and stepped away from the door. His eyes on Hester, he sidestepped to the table and fumbled the phone from its charger. It slipped between his fingers and crashed to the floor.

"Be careful," Irwin said.

The boy snatched it up. He held it against his chest, cradling it like a stuffed animal.

"Alright. Good. You did good. Now. Toss it up."

The boy didn't move.

"C'mon."

Nothing.

"Toss me the phone." Irwin stepped toward him. "Boy..."

"Bobby."

"Huh?"

"My name." He cleared his throat. "Bobby."

"Alright, Bobby. Toss the phone up."

"Is she really—?"

"Give me the goddamned phone!"

Bobby threw the phone. It sailed through the air, spinning end over end, Bobby darting out the door, Irwin holding the rail with one hand and reaching out with the other, stretching, trying to—

The phone landed in Hester's lap with a dull thump.

God.

Dammit.

Irwin sighed.

It was right there. All he had to do was take it from her lap, reach past her blood on the wall, past the place where her face had once been, reach into the blood-speckled fabric of her dress and grab the phone.

Easy, he told himself. So easy.

He took several deep breaths, closed his eyes, and thought of the way her cruel laugh echoed through the house.

"You are such a monumental pussy," she'd said when he found what she'd done to his charcoals. "Just a grade-A fucking wuss."

He'd glared at her, felt the heat rising in his face, felt something primal and ugly bubbling up his throat.

She had sensed it, too, and stepped forward, shoving her face into his. And she grinned. Goddammit, she *grinned*.

"Do it," she said. "I know you want to. Fucking hit me."

He did want to. He wanted to hit her so badly. Irwin hated himself for that.

"Pussy," she said again and laughed.

He reached out, snatched the phone from her lap, and hurried back up the stairs.

Easy.

"Ha!" He said. "I beat you! Do you hear that, Hester? I fucking beat you!"

He danced in a little circle at the top of the stairs, something akin to an Irish jig. He laughed wildly and thought he must look like some sort of demented leprechaun.

"I. Beat. You," he said again and thrust a finger toward her.

Pressing the button on the phone, he thumbed the screensaver away.

He stared at the screen a moment, confused. Had she done something to his phone? This wasn't his home screen. It looked like...

"Oh, no."

A security prompt instructed him to place his finger on the sensor. He hadn't setup a lock on his phone, had never felt the need. He sure as hell had never scanned his fingerprint into it before.

"Oh, no," he said again, realizing that Bobby had not grabbed *his* phone from the table.

And the only way to unlock Hester's phone was with her fingerprint.

Irwin looked down to where she sat, her hand on the floor, blood running down her arm and trailing from her thick fingers onto the stair.

The phone slipped from his hand, bouncing once before tumbling off the side of the staircase. He heard it shatter on the ground below.

He leaned over the rail to see shards of black plastic and metal scattered across the floor.

"Shit," he said.

Inhaling slowly, he turned back to Hester.

"Well. Alright, then."

He turned toward his room where he would open the window and yell for help like some child. That was all he could do, now. The heaviness inside him would allow nothing else. She had been right about him, after all. He had again tried and again failed.

Do not mistake my weakness for kindness.

"You win."

He paused in the bedroom doorway. From this angle all he could see were pale, fleshy legs and the light reflecting from her anklet. It looked as though she leaned back against the wall, relaxing. Content. Her pain finally at an end.

"You win," he said again and opened the window.

BIOLOGY

If Elmer had known how Tuesday was going to end, he might have played sick and avoided climbing on the school bus altogether. But he didn't and so he found himself in Mrs. McCafferty's third period Biology class watching a poorly made video about hormones and chemicals in the brain.

Violetta Deveraux sat next to him and the smell of her perfume, an exotic scent he imagined to be French and filled with magic and desire, drifted over him. He glanced at her as she scribbled notes and wished that he was brave enough to tell her how he felt.

"Oxytocin is often called the 'love hormone,'" a cartoon bear said as it pointed at a photograph of a molecule, "due to the feelings of desire and attachment its production creates."

Elmer had been in love with Violetta since seventh grade, when the two of them sat next to one another in Social Studies. Her gentle lips and fragile eyes and cascading brown hair whispered promises to him that he had only begun to understand. Even now, a freshman at Douglas MacArthur High, he couldn't quite grasp her hold over him.

"Pheromones," the bear said, "send unconscious messages through the air from one animal to another member of their species. These chemicals typically convey messages about sexual readiness."

He had asked her out once, asked her if she wanted to hang out that Friday night after he had made her laugh in Spanish class, and she had said yes. Proud beyond belief, he bragged to his friends about it. He was high, higher than he'd ever gotten from smoking up with Carlos Larkin in the back of his dad's rusted out pickup truck. He promised himself he'd tell her when they were together that he loved her.

That night Violetta had called him to explain, with a sweetness and kindness that broke his heart, that she didn't realize he'd been asking her out and had thought he'd meant they should hang out as friends. For some sick reason he didn't understand, this made him love her all the more. Still, he said nothing.

"Testosterone is the primary male hormone," the bear said. "It's responsible for focus, confidence, sexual urges, aggression, and competitive behavior."

A sharp pain shot through his ear. Elmer sucked in a quick breath and whirled around. Derrick Carruthers, baseball player, rich kid, and all-around asshole, sat behind him.

"Eyes front, Elmer Fudd." Derrick nodded toward Violetta and Elmer's worst fears were confirmed.

They were dating.

He'd heard the rumors. Everyone had. But until he had proof, he'd dedicated himself to abject refusal.

Not that Derrick needed a reason to be cruel to him. After all, Derrick had been responsible for smashing Elmer's nose in eighth grade ("Oops," he'd said after head butting Elmer. "I slipped."). He had been the mastermind behind breaking into Elmer's locker and scattering his things all over the track at the beginning of the year. He had held Elmer down in the bathroom while Kurt Robeson and Andy Maklin pissed on the crotch of his pants.

Yet the way he nodded toward Violetta said volumes more that Derrick would ever be capable of saying himself.

Elmer glanced at her, warmth flooding his cheeks at the thought she might have noticed him watching her. But her focus remained on the screen ahead as she chewed on the end of her pencil.

"Epinephrine is the fight-or-flight hormone. It's responsible for metabolic shifts and priming the sympathetic nervous system for action."

Elmer's cheeks had grown ridiculously hot. He looked down at his book and wondered how silly his fat little face looked right now, his chipmunk cheeks blazing red all the way up to his messy, greasy hair. The thought of it made him even more embarrassed, made the heat worse.

Fucking Derrick. That asshole was a disease that lingered in his blood, waiting for the most inopportune moment to strike, to bubble up and bring Elmer down.

"Both a hormone and a neurotransmitter, epinephrine increases the heart rate and the rate that the lungs bring oxygen into the blood stream."

The anger he felt at Derrick made him hotter, redder he knew. This in turn embarrassed him more which made him hate Derrick more, and on and on and on. His blood churned inside of him and scorched the walls of his arteries.

"We're nothing but chemicals and hormones," a wily old toad in a cowboy hat said. "Everything we feel inside of us, it's all biology."

Derrick flicked the back of his ear again.

Elmer whirled. The heat inside of him was too much. It needed to break free.

The asshole's eyes went wide looking at him. Elmer wondered if it was because of the hot tears he felt streaming down his face.

"Elmer," Violetta's soft voice whispered next to him. "You're bleeding."

The blood swelled against his eyes, scalding them, before gushing out the corners and down his face. Sweat bubbled up all over his skin, only it wasn't sweat, it was too hot and too thick and too sticky.

Derrick scooted back in his seat, other kids staring now. "Elmer, dude..."

His pores split and burst and erupted, boiling blood shooting out in torrents onto the asshole. Derrick screamed and the smell of bacon burning in its own fat filled the air. Elmer stood and stepped toward his tormentor, other people screaming, running, fighting to leave. The blood kept pouring out of him, shooting onto Derrick's smoking, twitching corpse, dissolving him, devouring him.

For the first time in his life, Elmer felt powerful.

He spun, his body no longer there, simply his fluids, hot boiling blood hanging in a vague boy-shape and filled with hormones, with epinephrine and testosterone and oxytocin, the air around it heavy with pheromones.

Violetta sat stunned, shocked, tears in her eyes and her jaw hanging loose.

"I love you," Elmer gurgled.

And then he washed over her.

WHERE CARRION GODS DANCE

The lid squeaks open and the smell claws at my face. I turn away, eyes watering, the odor old garbage and roadkill. Three fat flies buzz from the box, zipping around frantically before exiting through the living room window.

Holding my breath, I lean forward and peek inside.

Pitch black.

I pull my desk lamp closer, but the black doesn't dissipate. It takes a few seconds more before I realize it's hair.

There's a head in this box.

Jolting backwards, I tumble from my chair, my foot catching on the desk and flipping it over. Everything takes flight: pencils, papers, laptop. And, of course, the head. It hits the floor with a wet thump. It doesn't roll, as I imagined it would, but simply sits where it fell, one cheek pressed into the ground.

Lying on my side, staring into its face, I see that its eyes are gone, the eyelids with them. The lips have been sewn shut, the nose ragged as though it's been gnawed on. Its ears are deformed, almost like the cauliflower ears wrestlers get. The black hair is long and stringy and drapes onto the floor.

I've got to call the police. Where did the damned phone get thrown to? Scanning the room, I see it lying on the floor beside the head.

Of course.

I reach for the phone, stopping when I see the thing's ears. They aren't broken or mangled. No, they've been stapled shut.

You poor bastard. Some monster sewed your lips

together, stapled your ears closed, and cut your eyes out before sawing your head off. What kind of bizarre shit happened to you?

I'd first seen the box on the side of the road on my way to work Monday. It was white, about two feet square, and I'd said to myself, "I wonder what's in there?" A blip of thought on another bland beginning to another bland day in the accounts receivable department. It's not satisfying work by any stretch of the imagination, but it pays the bills. The paycheck is the only thing that gets me through the day. I spend four hours before lunch logging payments into the computer, and four hours after lunch returning calls to customers who are pissed-off about their billing cycles. My lunch hour is spent eating a tuna sandwich and watching Dr. Oz. This has been routine for so long that I have a hard time remembering what life was like before it.

I saw the box again on Tuesday. And then Wednesday. I passed it twice a day, to and from work, and each time my curiosity grew. Could it be something valuable? I fantasized about bank robbers having to ditch a bag of hundred-dollar bills because the police were in pursuit. Or some collector who hadn't noticed the box filled with Confederate coins bounce from the back of his truck. Anything could be inside of it and I couldn't stop wondering.

Halfway home Thursday, the curiosity got to me and I pulled onto the shoulder of the road, rain coming down hard as I pulled the hood on my jacket up and climbed from the car. On my side of the guardrail, in the waist-high grass, the box sat waiting.

I waddled over to it, my now-wet pants sticking to my thighs. It shouldn't have been as visible with the grass so high, but its white sides winked through the brush like a beacon. It made a loud sucking sound as I pulled it from the mud. It was heavier than I had expected, the material course and scratchy. I placed it on a tarp in my trunk, trying not to get mud all over everything, and sped home.

So here I am now, wondering where the box came from

as I slide a pair of old work gloves on. Lifting the head from the floor, I place it gently on my desk. Its skin is soft, like felt. The wet stub of a neck clings to the wood and keeps it from rocking over.

I pull my chair back up and stare at this thing. The smell doesn't bother as much now, so I examine it. I don't know why, but how many opportunities will I ever have to do something so out-of-the-ordinary?

This is probably why I'm divorced.

The skin, a sickly pale green, wrinkles a little around the eye sockets and mouth. A clump of the thin hair falls out when I touch the spongy scalp. The eye sockets are jagged, like someone really had to dig to get the eyes out. The purple lips have been sewn together with fishing wire. I poke the cheek and one of the staples pops loose on the ear.

Grabbing some pliers from the garage, I remove the staple. Somewhere in my mind I realize this is probably a crime, tampering with evidence or something, but the curiosity is too strong. There are five staples in each ear, and I pull each one out slowly, trying not to damage the tissue. When I'm done, the ears unfold partly, just enough for some sort of brown liquid to leak out.

I swallow the bile rising in my throat and head toward the kitchen to grab a roll of paper towels for the mess when I hear the moaning.

My gaze shifts to the television, but I realize I'd never turned it on.

The moaning is coming from the head.

I look closer, knowing I have to be wrong about this, knowing it's impossible and thinking some kind of animal maybe burrowed its way into the skull, some mouse or bird that's trying to get free.

The lips twitch.

Outside. Now.

Fresh air, that's all I need. It can't be good for you to smell decomposing flesh for too long. That's got to induce some kind of hallucination or something, right? I just need to clear my head a little. Walk around the block a few times.

I return an hour later and tip toe inside. It's dark now and the only light on in the house is my desk lamp. It shines like a spotlight on the head. The room is silent, no more moaning.

I approach slowly, ready for the lips to twitch again.

Nothing happens.

Now I know I was hallucinating. I grab some paper towels and wipe up the brown goo, thinking about how I should call the police and get rid of this rotting piece of meat and bone that's fouling up the air and killing my brain cells. I know this is what I should do.

So, when the moaning starts again, why do I grab wire cutters from the garage?

The fishing line snips away from the lips and the moaning stops.

The jaw creaks open. It looks like it's yawning. I'm breathing heavily as I slump onto the couch as far from the head as I can get and still be able to see it.

"I know you're here," it says. "I can hear you breathing." The thing's voice is sweet, like a child's. Its lips and jaw barely move when it speaks, the voice sounding like it's coming from the other end of a long, hollow tunnel.

"Please speak to me," it says.

The leg of my pants grows warm, and I absent-mindedly realize that I just let go.

"Who...What are you?" I don't know what else to say.

"Who are you?"

"Randy. My name is Randy."

"You found me, Randy. You let me speak and hear again."

"Who did that to you?"

"They all do, Randy. And you will too. Few can bear to hear what I have to say."

I turn on all the lights in the house and grab a knife from the kitchen, just in case. I don't know what a severed head could do to me, but I'm not taking any chances.

"And what exactly do you have to say?" I ask as I turn on the overhead light in the dining room.

"You'll hear it, when the time is right."

The smile fades and the jaw goes slack again.

I wait for it to continue, but there's nothing more.

I sit on my couch for the next hour staring at the head and wondering if this could all be real. I try to talk myself into calling the police, but I can't figure out what would I tell them.

At some point, while contemplating the horrid absurdity of it all, I fall asleep on the couch. The dreams are mostly about work, but some are about Carol. I dream of her tied to a chair somewhere, staring at a computer screen, desperately trying to return my Facebook messages. In reality, I've messaged my ex-wife once a week for the past month. She never writes back. I try not to care, but the dream alone proves my failure at apathy.

Music startles me awake and I reach to turn my bedside alarm off before I realize I'm on the couch. It's not an alarm.

It's the head.

And it's singing.

Wiping my eyes, I sit up to look at the thing. Its lips and jaw twitch awkwardly, but the voice coming from inside is perfectly angelic. It's such a bizarre scene, this eyeless, severed head sitting on my desk singing to me, that it takes a minute to puzzle out the song. "Imagine" by John Lennon.

The cherubic voice fills the room like a macabre Bose system. It's sweet and beautiful and chills my blood.

When the song is finished, it falls silent. I ask it to sing again, but it just sits there as mute as you'd expect it to be.

The next morning, I'm an hour late for work. I feel sluggish, like lead is pumping through muscles made of concrete. I rush out the door without even eating, hoping that Brenda in customer service has brought donuts again.

I refuse to look at the head as I leave.

My project manager immediately calls me into his office

and gives me shit for my tardiness. I've been punctual for five straight years, but today I get completely reamed. After that bullshit, I try to work, but all I can think about is the head. I doodle it inside doodles I'd done yesterday of the box.

At around noon, I get a phone call. I'm surprised to see that it's Carol. My heart pounds its way up into my throat. We exchange pleasantries and I ask her if she's gotten my messages.

She sighs and pauses and then tells me the "good news."

"I'm getting married," she says. "I wanted to tell you myself."

I don't know how to respond to that. It seems like just yesterday that we were married, that we bought a house, that she was pregnant. It seems like only yesterday that she had a miscarriage, that we fought constantly, that I found out the baby hadn't even been mine.

I say "Congratulations" and find an excuse to get off the phone.

When lunchtime rolls around, I realize I forgot to pack mine, so I have a candy bar from one of the vending machines. I sit down and turn on the television only to find that the cable's out.

I eat my candy bar alone and in silence.

After lunch, I sit back down at my desk. I imagine that I'll spend the rest of the afternoon thinking about the head, but I don't. I spend it thinking about Carol. Carol getting married again. Carol buying a new house. Carol making love to some other guy. I even doodle her getting it from behind. She's on all fours with her hands propped on either side of the box. The guy fucking her has his hands on her hips and he's insanely muscular, a steroid dealer's wet dream. He doesn't have a head.

The box says "Imagine" on the side.

I stay an hour late to please my boss, only to find out he's already left for the weekend. On my way home, I grab some slop from a drive thru. I pull into the garage, shut the door behind me, and sit down at my desk.

The head doesn't seem to notice.

It's not fair. Carol is the one who cheated on me, the one who refused to go to counseling. She gets to move on with her life, but I'm still stuck in the same goddamn place as when she left me. I haven't so much as gotten a handjob since the divorce, while her new hubby is boyfriend number three. They're probably eating dinner at some snooty French restaurant, nibbling on hundred-dollar steak with cream sauce as a waiter named Francois extols the virtues of Pinot Noir. Meanwhile I'm snarfing down fast food in front of a severed head.

Jesus, why do I still have this thing?

I rip the paper from around the burger and the smell hits me: french fries, stale buns, fried meat-like patty, processed cheese-like product, grease, and rot. Oddly enough, the smell from the head almost adds to the flavor of it all.

I finish eating and recline in my chair. I feel full, satiated. It's a trick of the fast food, I know. In five minutes, I'll be sick and bloated and greasy. For now, though, it feels good.

"Do you want to know what she's doing right now?"

It's the head. Or the voice from inside the head. I haven't made up my mind if the voice belongs to the head or simply uses it to speak. The mouth moves some, but not enough to form the syllables.

"What *who's* doing now?" I ask.

"Carol. You can listen, if you'd like."

The jaw drops again and hangs loose.

Is this possible? Can this thing actually let me eavesdrop on her? And, if it can, do I really want to know?

Finally, I wipe a greasy hand down my face and say, "Sure."

A sigh issues forth from the thing's mouth as though it's irritated at the answer. I start to get angry. After all, *it* asked *me* if I wanted to listen.

Then it does it again and I recognize the sound.

Not this. I don't want to hear this. Anything but this.

It does it once more and I'm positive. It's the sound of Carol having sex.

I want to tell it to stop, that I'm done listening, but I can't. I want to hear this, *need* to, the same way I sometimes pick scabs off before they're done healing. I'm not through with the pain yet.

Her sounds become more heated. Gasps for breath.

I've missed that.

She moans slightly, whispers, "Oh, yes. God, yes." It's Carol's voice, pure and unfiltered, as though her lips are against my ear.

The mouth on the head hangs open, unmoving.

"Mmmmmm... Oh, yeah. Right there. Yes. Yes! Oh, God."

I can't pull myself away, listening to Carol take it from some stranger who makes no sound whatsoever. I can almost smell her, that light scent of her sweat and the lavender soap she uses and some expensive shampoo I can't remember the name of. Her voice in my ear, it's almost as though she's straddling me now. There's a dull ache in my crotch and I close my eyes, remembering: her naked body, so small and slim; her tiny, perky breasts; her moist, thick lips and the way that she would bite her lower one when approaching climax; her bony little hips and the red peach fuzz of pubic hair.

Her voice gets louder—"Oh, God, yes, yes! Right there. Oh, Jesus, fuck me!"—and I pull myself out, almost feeling her mouth wrap around me. I remember the way her skin tastes, that salty sweet taste of sweat and body lotion. I grunt and moan and gasp for air as she starts panting, quicker, quicker. The pitch of her voice gets higher and her breathing even faster, so fast I wonder how her heart and lungs don't explode from the pressure. She's saying something, calling out a name, and I say, "Oh, Carol" before we climax together.

Silence.

In the quiet, I try to remember what it felt like to lie next to her, to hold her, to cuddle her, but all I can feel is the wetness already going cold on my hand and thigh. I still hear her voice in my head, panting and moaning and calling out—

Calling out "Brian." Calling out the name of her soon-to-be husband.

I open my eyes and there's the head, stock still and silent on my desk.

I rush to the bathroom. Slam the door. Lock it. I wipe myself up and then take a shower, the water steaming hot and damn near blistering my skin. I feel ashamed and disgusted. I feel dirty and filthy and jealous. I feel angry and sad and aroused. I feel all these things and yet feel nothing at all.

Unable to look at the thing on my desk again, I go straight to bed.

I cry myself to sleep.

The next morning I'm awake at seven but fight to go back to sleep. I'm dreaming of Carol, of course, and I don't want to leave the fantasy. Except when I slip back into the dream it all changes, morphs into a nightmare orgy, Carol fucking twenty or thirty strangers as I just sit and watch.

When she's done, she walks over to me and cradles my face. She smiles and kisses me on the lips. I can taste every one of those men.

As she pulls away, I notice the fishing line stitched across her throat.

I wake again around noon when the head starts laughing.

I storm into the living room and yell, "What the hell's so funny?"

And then it turns to face me.

The head somehow pivots on the table, leaving a greasy streak underneath it. Hollow holes stare toward me and I know, I just *know* the thing is looking at me. Its jaw drops open and it mutters something, something incomprehensible. It takes a moment to catch the pattern. It's not just gibberish. I don't know what language it is, or what it means, but it keeps speaking.

"Gochanwn gochenyn wythgeith. Pan elei dy dat ty e helya."

There's a sing-song quality to it, like a children's nursery rhyme.

When it's done, it laughs again.

"I just remembered that one," it says.

I slump down in the chair in front of it. It rotates back to its original position and faces me, jaw hanging loose.

"What's it mean?" I ask.

"Nothing important. Something about your father's spear."

I hesitate before asking it anything else. Should I encourage its ramblings?

"What else do you know?" I ask, knowing the question is a dangerous one. "What else can you tell me?"

I can't help it. I have to know what else there is. What other secrets this thing knows, secrets about Carol. Secrets about anything.

"Are you certain you want to know?"

It sounds almost like it's being coy.

"Yes. Yes, please tell me."

"If you truly wish to know, I will tell you everything."

"Yes, please!"

And it does.

When it's finished, I quickly sew the lips shut again. I staple the ears closed and wrap the entire head in aluminum foil. I put it back in the box, put that box in another box, and throw it into the trunk of my car.

I grab the small, black case that sits in the top of my closet and throw that in, too.

It's been days since it started answering my questions. I don't know how many, but I'm hungrier and sleepier than I've ever been. Eating and resting can wait. I must get rid of this thing. Take it as far from here as I possibly can.

I try to push the things it told me out of my mind with other, purer thoughts. Thoughts of my childhood or my wedding day or Christmas. It's no good. What it said keeps sliding back into my mind like a tidal wave of blood and shit and every foul thing that has ever been and ever will be. Its voice has birthed worlds of torment in my ears that I will never free myself from.

It told the story in reverse, God knows why. I can only suppose it has a sense of drama and wanted to save the most horrendous events until the finale. It started with the end of everything. That will be soon, from what it said, and horrible beyond imagining.

Then it switched midstream, from global to personal. It told me how Carol had cheated on me throughout our marriage, before even, and not just the time I knew about. She had problems, it said, problems I had no inkling of. A stepdad who touched her in places he shouldn't have, a mother who turned a blind eye. It named every man who had been inside of her and told me how she liked to take it in the ass from some of them. On three separate occasions she'd even had two men at the same time. It told me it knew I wanted to be above such petty things, that I wanted to be progressive in my ideas of a woman's body and her sexuality, but it also told me it knew my conservative upbringing wouldn't allow that and the pain of knowing all this would never stop eating at me.

The baby, oddly enough, *was* mine. The head was certain of this. It said that Carol was, too, and that's why she ended the pregnancy. She couldn't stand the thought of it, bringing a child into this world, and lied to me about the miscarriage. It said I reminded her too much of her stepfather. It was my eyes, it said, and the way I laughed. In a perverse way, it was what had attracted her to me in the first place.

Then it went farther back. In a great, booming voice, the kind I imagine Greek orators used to tell the teeming masses about mythological monstrosities, it related every grisly detail of my father's suicide and of his disappointment in me. How my sister hadn't really run away at sixteen but had been picked up by a truck driver when she was hitchhiking home. She'd been left to rot in a pile of mulch three counties away. The coyotes made sure that there wasn't enough of her to identify.

Then farther back. The atrocities in Cambodia, the Holocaust, the Rape of Nanking. Old Macdonald had a farm. God. Damn. Him.

Then farther, making sure that I knew every gory detail of the Crusades and of the Roman sack of Carthage. I think that's in Tunisia.

Tunisia. Africa, right? Why?

Farther still, revealing that all religion was a lie cooked up to hide the truth of the awful things that actually birthed the world into being.

No. That's not right. Is it?

"Birth" isn't the right word. That's the problem. They *shit* the world into existence and humanity has suffered ever since. We are their waste. It showed them to me, just a glimpse, and I could feel parts of my brain wither and die rather than process what it had seen.

What it had seen.

It told me so many things, too many for me to even relate. I was shown the beginnings of life and the universe and it was the basest, most vile thing I've ever seen.

That goddamn fucking word again!

My eyelids are falling closed like fire doors, and I keep snapping them open, snapping them open, snapping them open. I can't sleep until this thing is gone. I have to keep driving, driving, driving. I don't know where to yet, but I know I'll recognize it when I see it. The thing should be burned, smashed open, chopped into little pieces, but I know that none of that will work.

It told me so.

And, God help me, I know everything it told me is true.

I drive for hours. I drive past sunset. I drive past

thunderstorms. I drive past the world, leaving behind all the goodness and beauty that existed there, all the things I never experienced. I leave myself there, somehow. I weep openly as I drive past farms and forests, past mountains and rivers. I drive until I don't see light in any direction. No streetlights, no headlights, no corpselights. Nothing.

Nothing?

Rivers of shit.

I stop the car and get out. This looks like the place where carrion gods dance.

I take the box from the trunk and place it on the ground, my ground, my black case coming out to sit beside it. There's a gardening spade in my trunk. I take the box from the trunk and place it on the ground, my ground, my black case coming out to sit beside it. There's a gardening spade in my trunk and this looks like the place where carrion gods dance. I take the box from my trunk—

FOCUS!

I start digging. The ground is hard and rocky, but I must keep digging, digging, digging. The muscles in my arms are pumped full of white-hot lava, threatening to burst I'm digging so fast. Finally, the spade snaps in two.

I guess this will do. Not deep enough, it could never be deep enough. But it will do.

I take the box and place it in the hole. When it's covered, I pat the dirt down until it's nice and even.

Then I open the black case and stare at what's inside.

Maybe all our problems come from glimpses of the horrible, awful truth of everything. When we dream, it told me, we brush up against the ones who dance. Maybe we hear things we don't remember upon waking, things that are too much for the mind to dwell on. But how could I not dwell on them? How could I know the truth and not have it eat away at me?

It told me I would come to this place, that I would do this. That must also be true, then.

So why wait?

I pull the gun from the black case and place it into my mouth.

At least this one act that I do will make Carol happy.

For a time.

I sent her a message before leaving, just as the head instructed. She'll find me here, and she'll weep, but in the end, she'll be glad that I'm gone. One last albatross from around her neck.

But she will dream of me and wonder why I came all the way out here to do it. Wonder why I had that dirt covered spade in my hand.

Then, one night, maybe years from now, she and Brian will fight, and he'll say awful things and she'll leave him and their new baby and take these dark roads herself, coming back to the place where I ended myself. She'll stand here and, unsure exactly why she came, she'll think of me and she'll cry.

Then she'll dig.

THE THOUSANDTH HELL

"You should have been aborted," my old man said and smacked me hard enough to grind the broken glass into my gums. "It wouldn't have been an ordeal. You had an older brother I ended with a coat hanger when I was fifteen. I heard that girl could never have children again. But two years later when I met your mother, I could have made dong quai strong enough to turn you into little more than harsh cramps and a messy three days."

He grabbed a stick from the fire burning next to us and crouched against a pole. The orange light cast dancing shadows across his face and illuminated a charred hand, little larger than an infant's, that still wriggled as it smoked on the end of the stick. Moans echoed in the darkness and when I squinted, I thought I could make out taller poles deep in the black, shapes squirming on them as they slid down.

My father took a wet bite from the hand, blood and black ash staining his mouth. As he smacked his jaws together tiny bits of gristle dripped down his chin.

"The food here isn't as bad as you'd think." He laughed. "I've been wanting to ask you... "

I spit a fistful of blood and glass onto the ground. The cracked earth drank it in. "Ask me what?"

"What's been the worst for you? So far, I mean."

"Other than having to see you again?"

He tugged on the chain piercing my bowels and my insides threatened to unravel.

"The maggots," I said when the pain eased, and I caught my breath.

He laughed again. "Not the boiling oil? For me it was the boiling oil."

I shrugged. The Hell of Boiling Oil had been a lifetime ago. The burning tickle in my organs from the Hell of Burrowing Maggots was much fresher.

He thrust a thumb behind him. "Wait until you get to the Hell of Upside-Down Sinners. Those people are not happy."

Some say Fengdu consists of Eighteen Hells. Others, Nine Hundred and Ninety-Nine. Buddhist, Taoist, Hindu, and Confucian teachings about the afterlife all seemed to be true, even where they contradicted one another. Even the Maoists and Christians had gotten a few things right. And, of course, there were surprises for even the most theologically minded. The result was a never-ending panoply of torments with no clear path on how to rise above it.

"What do you want?" My gums still ached when I spoke.

He wiped the mess from his mouth with his forearm. "I wanted to see you."

"To gloat?"

"It's part of my punishment," he said.

Seeing as I was the one on a leash, I couldn't help but laugh. "Part of *your* punishment? How so?"

"Knowing what I did to you." He stared at his shoes. "Our ancestors are not pleased at how our line ended."

"Not pleased with me, you mean." Here I was, dead for God knows how long, and I still felt like a disappointment.

"They blame me," he said. "You were my responsibility. I went wrong somewhere."

"You can say that again."

He yanked on the chain and I passed out.

When I came to, he was crouched low, hands moving in and out, breathing deeply.

"Buddha breathing hands?"

"It helps to focus," he said.

I climbed to my knees. The chain was wrapped around my waist. Aside from the festering knot of pus-filled flesh it poked out from, it could have been a belt.

"You should try it," he said.

"I don't know how."

"That's a lie. I taught you. When you were young, we'd do it together. Those are some of my favorite memories."

"They're some of my worst." I stood and stretched. "That's why I don't remember."

"You try hard to make your words like knives, Fei-chu."

"Yeah, Ba. I don't know why I would do that. You've always been so good to me."

"Chan Pou-soi," a voice rumbled like a rockslide.

"Ox-Head," my father said and stood.

The guard snorted. He glared at us, yellow eyes narrowing inside thick black fur, and slammed the end of his kwan do into the ground. The thick blade at its top caught the light of the fire and cast it back onto Ox-Head's red armor.

"His Imperial Highness, Majestic Overseer of Divine Cruelty and Keeper of the Ten Thousand Pains, Master of the Earth Prison and Judge of the Thirty-Six Courts of Hell, Yan Luo the Yama King requests your presence."

"And his too?" My father motioned to me.

"Bring the whelp."

My father unwrapped the chain and dragged me along like an obedient dog.

We stepped along a path of scuffed human skulls, the air thick with the suffering around us. Tiny bursts of flame lit up the sky here and there followed by the fluttering of paper as Hell Money rained down from the world above. Souls were released from their suffering long enough to snatch up the bills meant for them and hide them away. There was no use for the money here, but the act of burning it offered respite to the dead for the few blissful seconds it took them away from their torments. These small kindnesses were the only thing that kept some people going.

No one had ever burned money for me.

"Ba?" I asked.

"What?"

"Did you burn Hell Money for your father?"

"Yes."

"How often?"

"As much as I could."

"Did it help him?"

"I don't know. He was gone long before you sent me here." He shrugged. "But he was a good man."

We walked in silence for a long while.

"Fei-chu," he said as we neared the Hall of Butchered Hearts, "was I as bad a father as Devil Kwan said?"

"Yes." I didn't even pause.

The chain gained some slack.

Devil Kwan was the closest thing I ever had to a friend. He was also a pimp, a butcher, and psychotic in a way that frightened even the police. Yet he was one of the funniest and most vibrant people I ever met. Strange how that works.

We'd sit around Devil Kwan's apartment, getting high and contemplating our futures. He would go on and on about how one day he would be famous, a movie star or a politician. He was confident he had an important purpose in the universe.

I never had that confidence. I knew I would never amount to anything. Even then, I felt leashed to my father. My biggest fear had always been that my destiny was tied to his.

Walking through Hell, my chain in his hand almost felt natural.

In the Upper Kingdom are the Courts of the Celestial Bureaucracy where, so I've heard, statues of the Eight Immortals rise so tall it's impossible to see their faces. Crystal clear water pours from the bottom in magnificent fountains and any who drink from them can instantly relive the best moments from their life.

In contrast, here there are only the Faceless in Hell, horrendous creatures whose limbs bend in unnatural directions and cover their shapeless skulls with smiling Buddha masks. One of them scurried to us and ripped its mask away.

Its blank canvass rippled and shifted. My mother's tear-streaked face appeared, screaming at me. "Why did you let it all happen, Fei-chu? You've disgraced my memory and damned me to this place. Do you know what they do to me here?"

The tears came too fast and she leaned forward and licked them from my jaw.

The Buddha mask slid back into place and the Faceless scampered off to share my suffering with its pack mates.

Ox-Head sat us on long steel benches. A fire burned deep in the earth beneath them and it seared the skin of my thighs to sit. Yan Luo's court was dark, the stench of stale urine, feces, and burnt flesh filling the hall. The sounds of crying and vomiting echoed around us.

"I tried with you, Fei-chu."

I was quiet.

"Fei-chu?"

I ground my teeth together. My name had always been one of the primary reasons I hated my father. Who names their son Fat Pig?

"You should have obeyed me."

"You're a miserable old shit," I said.

"You heard your mother."

"That damned thing wasn't my mother."

He shrugged. "She'd still be ashamed of you."

I punched him in the jaw. He fell from the bench onto the floor, the chain pulled taut between us.

Someone behind us cleared their throat.

A small man stood at the end of the bench, long Imperial robes stretching to the ground, and clacked eighteen-inch fingernails together in front of him. "Please forgive my intrusion. Chan Pou-soi and Chan Fei-chu?"

"That's us," my father said. He stood and dusted himself off.

"This way, please."

We followed him deep into the black. I didn't know why the King of Hell had requested us, nor did I care. I suppose I should have been afraid, but I was too angry. Even with all the tortures I'd been submitted to, having to subjugate myself once more to my father, in any fashion, was the worst of all. If there was mercy in Hell, as the arhats claimed, then our time together would be over soon.

The temperature dropped in chunks as we made our way down into the black. The darkness was absolute, the way I imagine the depths of space to be, and all I had to go on was the direction my chain was pulled.

When I was young, my father forced us to walk behind him no matter where we went. My mother would shuffle along, head low, holding my hand and deferring to him in all things. The village they were from was a small one outside of Chongqing and they lived a life far beyond what most people considered "traditional." Growing up, my father was downright medieval in his mindset. The factory he worked for moved us to Hong Kong when it reverted to Chinese control and even there, on that bustling modern island, he forced the old ways on us while spending his evenings drinking and gambling mah jong with the Tonka boat people. I think he took to them more than anyone else because they lived such simple lives—backwards in my opinion—but pious and true to my old man. It was the will of Heaven to him and his new friends if a man neglected his family unless he was beating them.

"Did you get off on it?" I asked.

He snorted. "What are you babbling about?"

"Beating the shit out of us. Did that get you off?"

"You shouldn't speak to your father that way, Fei-chu. I never spoke to my father that way."

"The difference is you were scared of your father. I just hated mine."

"I did what I had to do."

"Right."

"And what should I have done, O Wise One? Should I have sat by while the urban cesspool around us corrupted you and your mother?"

"It's not corruption, Ba. It's progress."

"That's what they called the occupation of Shanghai and the Rape of Nanking. Progress."

"There's no talking to you, is there? There's just nothing rational going on in that hollow skull of yours."

The slap rang my head and left my cheek stinging and raw. "You will show me respect for once, Fei-chu. You never gave it to me in life and I'll be damned if you don't give it to me now." He turned and stepped away.

I grabbed my chain and jerked it back until I could feel my father's face in front of mine. "I respected you, you pathetic pig. I spent half my life respecting you. I only stopped when you proved you didn't deserve it."

"It was those friends of yours. Devil Kwan and his cronies. They ruined you."

"*You killed my mother.*" If I could have murdered him again, I would have done so right there.

The small man stepped beside us. "A thousand pardons, gentlemen, but Yan Luo does not like to be kept waiting."

We kept on through the black. The cold grew unbearable, my ears and the tip of my nose threatening to shatter to the floor.

One winter, my mother convinced the old man to let her and I go back to Chongqing to visit her family. He didn't like the idea, but her own father was ill and Ba at least paid lip-service to filial piety. The train ride west was one of my favorite memories. As soon as we left Hong Kong, a personality blossomed inside my mother. I had only known her up to that point as a slave to my father and a housekeeper to me, her mouth kept shut unless there was a lesson that needed to be taught or a question of my father's to answer. She showed me love and tenderness but always in a quiet way, with a hug or a bowl of soup and a pat on the head.

But on that train, shaking our way through the snow-dusted countryside, she sang to me. She had the most beautiful voice, and I was shocked I had never heard it before. Being away from my father, I felt I was seeing my mother for the first time. She told jokes that made me double over in laughter and taught me how to play poker and blackjack. We spent a month with her family high in the mountains and, while I had always loved my mother as a son should, I fell in love with her the way best friends do.

When it came time to head home, I hoped a transformation had come over her that she would carry back to Hong Kong.

As the train neared the city, she grew quiet and stared out the window. The woman she was fled like a ghost that only haunted the countryside, exorcised by the threat of my father's presence. There were glimpses of her true self after that, winks over dinner, a game of cards quickly played while Ba was out drinking, but she hid that side of her away like the money the old man won from the boat people and tucked inside a shoe box in his closet. She was a secret even to herself, a beautiful secret only whispered about when there was no chance anyone could overhear.

As I loved my mother more and more, I learned to hate my old man.

We were led into an opulent parlor of jade and ivory, red silk draped in long banners from column to column. Lanterns burned inside paper balls around the room. Our guide sat us on a gold sofa upholstered in red leather.

"Please wait here," he said and backed from the room.

Jasmine and incense accented the scent of untold wealth in the room. A bowl of oranges sat on a cherry-wood table next to us and I took one. It was velvety sweet and juicy and, for the first time since I died, I didn't feel like I was in Hell.

My father yawned beside me, a reminder that the torture was far from over.

Footsteps shuffled into the room. We turned as a

small group of men made their way in. Their dress ranged from the tattered rags of a farmer to the brown robes and wooden armor of a Han Dynasty soldier.

My old man fell to his knees and kowtowed.

Our ancestors eyed me as I remained seated, savoring the orange.

"Hey, Fei-chu." Devil Kwan plopped down beside me. "How you been?" His smile was as wide and inviting as it had always been and his dark, thick hair meticulously styled like he had just rolled out of bed.

I embraced him while my father stayed face down on the floor. "Kwan! What are you doing here?"

"I'm the new King of Hell."

"What?"

He laughed.

"What about Yan Luo?"

"Funny thing about that. Seems Yan Luo is a title instead of a name. Who knew?" He smacked my back. "Good to see you."

My head swam. This was all too much for me. "How did you...?"

"Turns out my cruelty is boundless. I always suspected it in life, but here in Hell? Man, once I was unleashed there was no stopping me. For a thousand years, my tortures were legendary. So, I was rewarded."

"Have we been here that long?"

He shrugged and picked a shred of pork from between his teeth. He sniffed it and sucked it down. "Who knows? Time doesn't mean much here. I've been here that long. You may have only been here a few days." He motioned to our ancestors. "Anyway, these guys are why I called you here."

"My ancestors, right?"

"Yeah. They're not much fun. They came down from the Celestial Courts to complain."

A Maoist soldier stepped forward. I think he was my grandfather, but I'd never met the man. "You two have ruined our line. Your impiety and resentment have dragged us all down."

"See?" Devil Kwan stood. He patted my father on the head like he was a mutt.

My old man creaked to his feet, eyes wide. "Father," he said to the soldier, confirming my suspicion.

My grandfather smacked him across the mouth. "You will not address me. You have disgraced me."

The Han soldier nodded. "Disgraced us all."

My father slumped onto the sofa next to me.

Devil Kwan grabbed an orange and leaned against the wall. He peeled it with one sharp fingernail. "These are good, huh?"

"What do we do now? How can we make amends?" My father looked to our ancestors, to Devil Kwan, to me. His jaw quivered and a tear leaked from his eye. It made me hate the man even more.

"That's the interesting part," Devil Kwan said. "Your souls must be scrubbed clean of all the baggage you carry. Weird, huh? It's like a buffet of beliefs down here." He laughed. "What do you hate the most, Chan Pou-soi?"

He looked at me and lowered his head. "My failure."

"And you, Chan Fei-chu?"

I stared at my old man and saw the night he beat my mother to death in a drunken rage. I saw the bribes he pulled from the shoe box when the police came. I saw the night I spent snorting lines with Devil Kwan, bitching about the old man, complaining about how we had no money, telling Kwan how much my father kept hidden in the house. I saw the old man rushing in and hitting me across the back with an iron bar, cash flying from the shoe box and across the floor, my knife catching the light as I plunged it into his gut over and over, his eyes wide, spittle flying from my jaw and onto his face, his blood soaking my hand. He clutched at me as the life fled from him and I laughed. Even when the firing squad cocked their rifles and readied to end me, the memory of that look in his eye made me laugh.

He had that same look now and I couldn't hide the chuckle.

"Him," I said. "I hate him."

Devil Kwan squeezed onto the sofa between us. He grabbed my chain and gently pulled it from under his ass. He took my hand, and then my father's, and smiled. "It's time for both of you to lose this weight you carry. It's time to be reborn."

My father exhaled and tears leaked down his face. "Thank you, oh thank you."

Devil Kwan winked at me.

His cruelty deserves its reputation. I never thought it possible, but arcane texts speak of rare individuals born with two souls. Two souls trapped together in one body, never able to escape one another.

As we prepare ourselves for being reborn, my father is optimistic. But I know that the suffering we've endured until now has only been a prelude.

Tomorrow, our true punishment begins.

THE LORD OF MISRULE

At an Inn outside Kilargh, Morgan said she didn't love her anymore. It was a hard thing for Siân to hear and made all the harder by how much time they still had left on this trip.

"It's not that I don't care about you," Morgan said while staring out the window at another gray Irish morning. "It's just not what it was."

"And what was it?"

"Wonderful," she said.

Siân had known this was coming, had hoped that by following Morgan she might postpone it, might even fix whatever had broken between them. Still, she couldn't keep the tears away.

"I'm sorry." Shoving her research material into a messenger bag, Morgan said they would talk more about it when she returned.

That was the last Siân ever saw of her.

☀ ☀ ☀

"We've searched the entire village," the Garda Sargent said. His name was Fitzgerald and he had a pale face, one eye constantly trembling as though it alone would cry. "From the river to the coast. We have volunteers out in the woods right now and I spent all morning on the grounds of that church."

"Then we should search it all again." Siân poured a cup of the Garda station's miserable coffee. "We've missed something."

Shaking his head, Fitzgerald reached around her to

grab a tea bag from one of the boxes on the counter. "What we've searched so far has taken us three days."

Tired of arguing, Siân sat at one of the small tables in the break room. They reminded her of the seating in an elementary school classroom and she couldn't quite get comfortable.

"Perhaps," Fitzgerald went on, "we need to talk about what's been staring us in the face."

"And what's that?"

"She's gone back to Connecticut."

"You found the rental car." It had been parked on the side of the road by a footpath leading to the church and returned to Siân after being searched. "And her bags are still in our room."

"If not Connecticut," he continued as though she'd said nothing, "then somewhere to get her head straight. To..." he trailed off.

"To get away from me." Her palsied hands sent coffee dripping down the side of the Styrofoam cup.

He sat across from her, the newly made cup of tea steaming on the table before him. The aroma rising from it made her think of wet, decaying leaves. "You said yourself, Miss Dennistoun."

"Misses."

"Aye. Sorry. Meant no offense. Just... Please look at this from my viewpoint. She tells you she doesn't love you anymore and then walks out the door."

"To continue her research. Just as she had every morning since we got to Ireland."

"And her research? What else can you tell me about that?"

"I told all of this to one of your officers."

"Aye. You did. Tell me now, then."

"Jesus." She laughed and wasn't sure why. "Okay. Sure. That church is the main reason we're here in Kilargh. We've been in Ireland about three weeks now. I thought

Coleraine was as far north as we could go, but then Morgan drove us here."

Siân had joked about the village "Welcome" sign proudly boasting fewer than eight-hundred residents. Morgan hadn't found that funny.

"This was the edge of Norman Ireland," Siân continued. "A few miles west of here was the seat of the ancient kings of Ui Neill. She's hoping to discover more about the clash between their two cultures."

"That's what she studies, then?" Fitzgerald asked. "Culture clash?"

"Norman Ireland. She's been here a dozen times."

"She must be great at her work. You been here a dozen times, too?"

"First time out of the States," she said and sipped her coffee. She wished she'd added more sugar, more creamer, more *something*, to offset the bitterness.

"First time? Truly?"

"Yeah. Why?"

"Your name, that's all. The spelling of it."

"My great-grandmother was Welsh." Morgan's family descended from Irish immigrants on her mother's side, though Siân didn't feel like exploring the psychology behind her wife's profession with the police.

He nodded and sipped his tea. "Morgan must do well. Financially, I'm saying. Be able to take a long trip like this."

"She's won a few grants. They cover the expenses."

Well, covered the expenses for Morgan, at least. Siân had been forced to sell her Toyota and quit the job at the bookstore in order to join her wife. She could get the job back when they returned Stateside and had hated the aging car more than she cared to admit, so the sacrifice wasn't as great as it seemed. Morgan's lack of enthusiasm when Siân announced she'd be coming along had hurt far worse.

"Something bother you about those grants?" He must have read the memory on her face.

"Hmmm? No. Not at all."

Fitzgerald stared at her in silence and she fought the urge to claw that trembling eye from his skull.

"Did you know about her arrests?"

"She's never been arrested."

"Aye. Three times."

"When? What for?"

"The first was when she a teenager and the record is still sealed, so I couldn't tell you the details. Though I was able to find out that the charge was arson."

Arson. Siân swallowed. That couldn't be true. Could it?

"Then, when she was twenty, she was arrested for breaking and entering. Report said it was the home of one of her neighbors and they ultimately dropped the charges."

"What was the third one?"

"That was just a few months later. Shoplifting. She nicked lingerie from a department store. That one did prosecute. She served thirty days in jail. She never told you any of this?"

"That was so long ago. We hadn't even met yet."

"Strange, though. That she never told you, I mean."

Siân shrugged. Morgan hid so much from her, it seemed.

"We'll keep the search up," he said and stood. "But we have Hallowmas coming and we'll be losing our volunteers tomorrow night. I'll call Coleraine and see how long we have their people for." He left the break room, the smell of his tea still lingering.

She'd almost forgotten tomorrow was Halloween. That surprised her. The lack of Halloween spirit had been one of the first things she'd noticed about Kilargh. The shops they'd passed that first day here were sparsely decorated, the odd orange and black streamer or plastic witch hanging but little else. Coleraine had been covered with so many Halloween decorations that she'd thought they were back in the States. She wished they'd stayed there.

"You'd think they'd at least have pumpkins out. I mean, they invented the holiday," she remembered saying.

"Halloween's more American than Irish at this point,"

Morgan had said. "Besides, in Ireland Jack-O-Lanterns are made from turnips."

"Huh. You learn something new every day."

"You might." Morgan had nudged her.

Laughing, Siân had put her an arm around her. "Your arrogance is almost sexy."

Ducking into a pub that first night in Kilargh to escape a cold rain, they laughed and drank until last call. It had been easy for Siân to forget that they'd come here for work rather than the honeymoon they'd never taken. When they'd made love that night, both drunk and giddy, it had reminded her of their first time together.

When she'd woken the next morning, Morgan had already left for the church.

Siân hadn't eaten all day, had felt too anxious to put anything inside of her, and when the woman who ran the Inn offered a bowl of stew, she almost turned it down. Knowing her evening Zoloft-Trazodone cocktail would nauseate her on an empty stomach, she took the bowl up to her room and ate while skimming through Lauren's notes.

Her wife had always been meticulous in research, recording every detail in the same kind of leather-bound notebooks she'd been buying since college. Opening one, the dry scent of paper made Siân feel as though Morgan were there in the room with her. A fat thumb print smudged the first page, likely the Garda officer's who had been going through Morgan's things. They hadn't found anything they could use. Even as detailed as her wife's research was, she had never been the type to keep a diary.

Siân wondered what exactly drew Morgan's attention to that church. The way Fitzgerald had described the place, it sounded small and inconsequential. Tucked away in the woods off the side of an unused road, he made it out to be an uninteresting ruin of moss-covered stone.

"Not even the teenagers go out that far," he'd said. "They find nearer places to fool around."

And yet Morgan had spent three days there before she'd gone missing.

Morgan had always had a wild streak in her. An odd trait for a scholar, to be sure, but she could be as impulsive and adventurous as anyone Siân had ever known. She had dismissed the arrests Fitzgerald had seemed so fixated on but now, alone in her room, they made sense. Morgan had never been one to accept the status quo. Look at this trip, scheduled as the result of some tiny, insignificant details her wife found in her research that excited her.

Or, perhaps, a better example might be how she had decided she was no longer in love and walked out the door, leaving Siân alone in a foreign country.

Where the hell could she be?

Siân's phone rang. It was her brother, likely calling for an update. She had nothing to share and that fact left her feeling hollow. She silenced the call.

Flipping through the notebook, she came across a rough sketch of a church at the top of one page. Morgan had never been a great artist, but the margins of her notes were always crammed with little illustrations. Siân thought she must have picked it up from all the years spent pouring over illuminated manuscripts.

Reading the page, she was surprised to find it a narrative. According to a note in the margin, it had been copied from "Legends of Northern Ireland," published in 1937.

During the reign of King John, Kilargh (then called An Áit Dóibh Siúd Tar, or The Place For Those Who Come) was the northern most village under Norman control. One of the ways the Normans asserted their culture in the region was by holding massive feasts and cementing a Norman type of worship in place of the local Christianity. These were immensely popular among the townsfolk, the most popular of which being the Feast of All Hallow's Eve. Every year during this feast, the Baron allowed the townspeople to appoint a Lord of Misrule.

The Lord of Misrule, a popular custom in France and England, would serve from Halloween until the Feast of Fools following Christmas. During his "reign," he would dress garishly in vibrant colors, often wearing masks and bells. He would be excused from any duties other than leading revelry and mischief which, more often than not, took the form of drinking and dancing.

A local mason named either Máelodor or Máeludir was said to have been chosen as the Lord of Misrule again and again. He was brother to the parish priest and had built the village church himself. The townsfolk and the Baron were both satisfied with the man for several years. Then, sometime during King John's reign, Máelodor disappeared. He was gone for a year and a day, returning three nights before the Feast of All Hallow's Eve. In their excitement, the people again appointed him as Lord of Misrule.

Máelodor's final appointment would end violently.

Her brother called again and, loneliness getting the better of her, she turned away from the notebook and answered.

"What time is it there? Did I wake you?" Aidan's voice quick and anxious.

"If you didn't want to wake me, you dick, why did you call twice?"

"I just assumed an intelligent person would have turned their ringer off."

She wanted to smile, but their usual banter felt forced tonight.

"There's still no news," she said.

"I'm sorry, Siân."

They both went quiet and she was glad. She didn't know what to say to that, was tired of responding to "I'm sorry" and "she'll turn up" and "don't give up hope."

"Do you think..." Aidan trailed off.

"Think what?"

"Just... I mean, after last time—"

"Don't start this, Aidan."

"I'm not. I just worry about you. And if Morgan took off again—"

"Not you too." Siân stood and walked to the window. She wanted to drive her fist through the glass.

"If Morgan did leave," Aidan went on, "you know you're welcome to stay here with us."

"She didn't."

Two middle-aged women stood in the dull yellow light of a streetlamp outside as they smoked. One glanced up at the window and nodded. The other followed her gaze, no doubt gawking at the American whose spouse had vanished.

"Did you tell the police about last time?" Aidan asked.

She backed away from the window. "No. Why would I? It's not the same."

"Siân. Come on."

"It's not. Last time was different, and you know it."

Last time had been after Siân quit grad school and folded in on herself. The pills she'd been taking then stopped working and there were several days where she couldn't even leave the bed. Morgan had been supportive at first, but after a few weeks her attitude changed. Always filled with a nervous energy herself, she couldn't understand why Siân was unable to be happy, why she couldn't laugh and joke and dance and do all the things that had made Morgan fall in love with her to begin with. Siân had tried to explain how it wasn't a choice, that she couldn't simply decide to come out of it, but by then her wife had had enough.

"You promised you'd finish grad school," Morgan had said while shoving clothes into an overnight bag. "Again, and again, you promised. I'm sick of you breaking promises. I'm sick of you always being on my ass. You're constantly here, constantly weaseling into whatever I'm doing. Why can't you get your own friends? Your own life?" She zipped up the bag and turned to glare at Siân. "Just because you gave up doesn't mean that I have to."

Siân hadn't responded to that, instead leaving the room to drink half a bottle of wine alone in the kitchen. She'd wanted to blame it all on her depression, wanted to say that she'd never been good at keeping promises, to say that grad school had never been her idea. But she didn't and Morgan had gone straight to the airport, taking the first international flight she could find. It had taken Siân weeks to discover she'd flown to Goa for one of the hundred Hindu festivals they held there each year. By then Morgan was back in the states and had blocked her calls.

"She came back," Siân said, her voice soft, almost pleading.

"Three months later." Her brother sighed theatrically. "I just don't like this hold she has over you. You'll follow her anywhere. Hell, you followed her halfway across the world and now look at things."

"Wow. That's finally something you and Morgan agree on."

"We made up the guest room," Aidan said, ignoring her response. "And the kids would love to see you. I'm looking at flights right now and—"

"Aidan. Please. I know you're trying to help, but this isn't what I need right now."

A pause. "Do you want me to come to you, then?"

She almost said yes. It would be comforting, sure, but she was afraid having her brother here with his jokes and off-color snark might improve her mood. Though she couldn't quite articulate it, she needed the hurt right now. She hoped that feeling didn't foreshadow another episode coming on.

"Nah. You'd just drink too much Guinness and get arrested for fighting."

"True." He laughed. "You sure?"

"Yeah. But thanks. I mean it."

"Well, the offer stands. And the other one, too. Like I

said, we've got a room made up for you here, so if you want to get some sunshine and eat something other than haggis, you're welcome to it."

"Haggis is Scottish."

"It's gross is what it is."

She laughed and they said their goodbyes. Yet when the call was over, she was worse somehow. Anxious. The room felt smaller. Cramped and hot. She wanted to go out into the cool night air. She wanted to run, to scream, to thrash about on the ground and pound her fists into the rocky soil.

She wanted a cigarette.

Grabbing her coat, she hurried downstairs, hoping the two women were still outside smoking. Siân had kicked the habit years ago (at Morgan's insistence) but on nights like this, when the stress was too much, she thought that no one ever really kicked their habits. They lingered like diseases, the symptoms flaring up when least expected.

The only signs the women had been there were flattened cigarette butts scattered across the ground. Siân leaned against the lamp post, her breath misting in the October night, and watched a man hang purple bats and fiery-eyed skeletons from the porch of a nearby house. He caught her looking and raised a hand in greeting.

Siân forced a weak smile and nod in return before walking down the street, a slight breeze dusting the air with the sour odor of mulch.

Torches rose six feet high and lined the path, casting deep shadows onto the red-bricked walls of suburban houses. Their orange glow flickered in the breeze and gave off the boggy smell of peat. She assumed they were for Halloween. Yet something about them seemed ancient and out of place.

The streets were empty, and she wondered what time it was. She hadn't bothered to glimpse at the screen on her phone before powering it off.

Glancing down a side street, she saw an old man closing

the gate to a small shop. Jackpot. It didn't take much to convince him to sell her cigarettes before he locked up.

"Can I also get a lighter or a matchbook?" she asked.

The shopkeeper slid two matchbooks across the counter to her. "On me," he said.

"Thanks, but I only need the one."

"What about your friend?" He motioned to the front door.

"Who?" Siân turned.

The street was empty.

"Oh," the old man said, a puzzled look on his face. "My mistake. I thought he'd been walking with you."

She thanked him and left. Lighting a cigarette, she was grateful for the rough, earthy taste. Focused on her re-acquired vice, she must have turned down a different street than the one she'd taken from the Inn. The torches were nowhere to be seen.

Back in her room, she brushed her teeth to dispel the taste of smoke even though her wife was not around to kiss her.

Trying to sleep, she lay in the dark until she couldn't stand it anymore. Clicking the bedside lamp on, she picked up Morgan's notebook again. It seemed somehow preferable to the novels she'd brought and, she had to admit, she was curious as to the violent end that Morgan's Lord of Misrule had come to.

Though the townspeople swore Máelodor had been gone for a year and a day, he himself insisted he had only gone for a stroll and hadn't been away more than a few minutes. This "lost time" is typical of much of the folklore of the era and usually attributed to encounters with the sidhe.

Following his return, Máelodor's revels took a much darker and chaotic bent. The dances and parties became orgies. Animal sacrifices were said to have been commonplace during this time and one story even relates how a local girl sold her virginity to any man willing to take her on the altar of the church Máelodor had once worked so hard to build. Men were said to run wild through the forest like beasts, leaving their lands uncared for, and women copulated with dogs and stags. People who left to dance at the church with the Lord of Misrule often disappeared themselves, never to be seen again. It is said he lured them to the other world to forever dance in his strange court. Women were the primary target of these disappearances and the folktales hazard all sorts of horrid guesses as to why.

Whatever the truth of the matter, Máelodor eventually led an army of revelers to the Baron's home. They butchered his household guard and family before dragging the Baron to the town's center and burning him alive in a massive bonfire. Máelodor ruled Kilargh as a true Lord for three years until agents of King John put down his rebellion.

Oddly enough, it was also on the Feast of All Hallow's Eve that Máelodor was put to death. Local legend says that his body vanished from the gallows before All Soul's Day, stolen by imps or faeries. The parish priest was also executed, as were a sizeable number of villagers. The village took a hundred years to recover its population and the violated church Máelodor had built wasn't re-consecrated until sometime in the mid-fifteenth century.

Siân now understood the interest in the place at least. Even disregarding the occult folklore, a little-known story of rebellion would have been precisely the kind of wild research Morgan salivated over. But what could still be at the church after all this time?

She read a few more pages of notes, surprised to find half a dozen more sketches of the church alongside a massive image of a horse's skull. The final page was filled with drawings of what looked like toadstools. A note was scribbled beneath them.

This world has gone gray and I crave color.

She wasn't sure if Morgan had copied the phrase from somewhere or if it had been her own. She wasn't even entirely sure what it meant, though something about it struck a nerve. It felt true to Siân in a way that made her stomach churn. It was a line she could have written herself in the worst bouts of her depression.

Exhaustion finally caught up to her and Morgan's perfect script began to blur. She sat the notebook down and turned off the light, thoughts of arson and shoplifting following her into sleep.

She parked on the side of the road and wondered if this was the same spot where police had found the car. The rain had slowed to a drizzle but she let the wipers continue their work, the rhythm of them on the windshield almost hypnotic. She was surrounded by dense forest, so much of it surprisingly still green amidst the reds and yellows. The autumn foliage may have been vibrant any other place, but here it seemed pale and sick. She blamed her mood for that as much as she did the weather.

Officer Broderick knocked on her window. She cracked it and rain streamed down onto her hand.

"You sure you want to do this? We've already been all over the wood here. Even had Mac Gannon's dogs out sniffing around."

She didn't answer, instead just rolled up the window and shut off the engine.

Broderick handed her a blue hooded tarp as she stepped from the car and she was glad. The rain was like ice pelting her face.

"This way," he said, and she followed him across the narrow road.

Young and gangly, Broderick moved with all the grace of a man stomping cockroaches. They forced their way through dense brush, and she was certain they would get lost.

Is that what had happened to Morgan?

"Any plans for Halloween?" Siân asked, feeling she should say something to the man after forcing him out in this weather.

"Not really. Might go to Sandra Murphy's party but watching scary movies on TV will likely win out. Folks have never been much for the holiday here. Not sure why. Just never took. We're a boring lot, we are."

They soon found the overgrown footpath, tiny stones rising from a floor of wet leaves every now and then as markers.

Broderick pointed to one. "Heard tell these things been here hundreds of years. No one would ever find the trail without them."

"Fitzgerald said that no one comes out here, not even teenagers."

Broderick laughed. "Well, as you can see, it's not the easiest of places to get to. We came out here once when I was in school. Me and some mates. That might have been Halloween, too, come to think of it. We thought we'd drink a little and smoke a little and talk about girls a lot. We never found the path, just ended up walking in circles for an hour until I fell and twisted me ankle. Then we gave up and left. Far more pleasant places to trek around to."

The path twisted through the woods, barren branches grabbing her tarp and threatening to rip holes in it with every turn. It wasn't long until they wound up a hill.

"Watch your step," Broderick said. "The trail gets steep in parts and when it's raining it's all too easy to slip."

"That how you twisted your ankle?"

"Caught me toe in a rodent hole. My mates joked it was the pooka trying to run us off."

"Pooka?"

"A local type of the fair folk. Malicious little shape-shifters." He laughed again.

Siân slipped on wet leaves and grabbed a tree branch to keep herself upright. "You mean like faeries?"

"As the stories go, this hill here is a faerie mound. They serve as a kind of doorway between our world and the other worlds. They're a favored place for the fair folk to come a calling. As the stories go."

"Is that why the church was built here? Kind of a way to cleanse the place?"

"I suppose so. Ah, here we are."

They crested the hill and stepped into a clearing. Short grass ran up to walls three feet high and pieced together from a random array of misshapen stones. The path, now stone rather than dirt, shot through a gap in the wall. On the other side of the clearing, the woods thick climbing another hill behind it, sat a small stone church. It looked like two distinct buildings had been wedged together. The first was short yet wide, the second tall and long. Each was rectangular in shape with a high triangular roof. A tower rose from the roof at the rear of it, a single window near the top.

"Why is this so hidden?" she asked. "You'd think it would be a tourist destination."

"This?" Broderick looked across the clearing at it. "Hundreds of these things dot the country. Every now and then some folks like your wife make the trek up here to take a peek, but they usually leave disappointed. You seen one tiny church, you seen them all."

He started for the church and she put a hand on his shoulder.

"Would it be okay if I went in by myself?"

Glancing at the church again, he said, "I suppose so. Just be careful. No one's used the place for at least a hundred years and that roof looks like it's going to come down any day now."

Following the path between the walls, a small cemetery came into view behind the church. There were maybe two dozen stones, most of them dark and squat and none looking as though any text was still legible. One Celtic cross stood in the center of the graveyard but even that, too, seemed crude and uninteresting. Perhaps Broderick had been right about this place.

The entrance to the church looked like a massive door had once been in place, but now there was simply an opening. As she stood there staring through the doorway, a feeling of being watched almost overwhelmed her. She looked to the forest, the trees and brush growing thick and tangled. No one was there. No one but Siân and the Garda officer, that is. She now wished she hadn't asked him to stay behind. But she had needed to see the place Morgan had spent so much time without others intruding. She dismissed the feeling of eyes on her as nerves and turned back to the building.

Leaves and twigs piled on the threshold and she stepped over them into the dark of the church. It smelled of mildew and old bones. Gray light trickled down from the rear of the structure (likely the window in the tower, she thought) but there were no other openings. She pulled her phone from a pocket and activated the flashlight app. The white light reflected from more spider webs than she was comfortable with. A fine layer of dirt covered the floor and one of the timbers from the roof lay rotting in the center. The walls were barren save for moss and no sculptures were visible. She tried to imagine the place with pews and tapestries and an altar but found it difficult.

Stepping over the fallen timber and thinking of what Broderick had said, she shined the light into the ceiling. Small pockets of shadow squirmed, and it took a moment to realize it was a bat colony. They were tiny creatures, almost cute as they nuzzled together.

A noise from the back of the church made her bring the light down.

There was nothing there, only the dull gray sun leaking onto a small puddle of rainwater on the floor. She wasn't even sure what the noise had been. It sounded like a bell jangling, but that couldn't be right.

Turning back to the entrance, a silhouette stood in the doorway.

"You were right," she said. "There's really nothing to see here but the bats." She looked down as she stepped over the piece of fallen timber. "At least one of them didn't swoop down and..."

The doorway was empty.

She hurried through it, suddenly not wanting to stay inside the church a second longer.

"Officer Broderick?" She looked around, uncertain where the officer could have gone, until she saw him standing where she left him by the wall on the other side of the clearing.

When she reached him, she told him what she had seen.

"Wait here," he said and jogged over to the church. He looked around the exterior before pulling a flashlight from his belt and stepping inside.

Once again, she felt as though someone watched her. She examined the trees surrounding the clearing, looking for a shape or movement of any kind.

The woods were still and quiet, the only sound the falling rain.

Broderick exited the church, replacing his flashlight on his belt as he jogged back over.

"I imagined it, didn't I?"

He laughed. "It is a bit spooky out here. But I'm glad you did."

"Why's that?"

"Because if you didn't, I would have never found this." He held up a clear evidence bag. Inside was a small, dark sphere.

"What is it?"

"A bell," he said.

That night was the first Halloween she'd spent without Morgan in over a decade. One of the volunteers had invited

Siân to Sandra Murphy's party but she wasn't sure if she'd go. It didn't feel right without Morgan. The holiday was their favorite time of year and, after spending an hour or two at whatever parties they could find, their ritual had been to curl up on the sofa with a bowl of candy and watch horror movies until they passed out from the sugar. It was one of the few times Morgan had seemed content to sit still.

The bell had been sent off to Derry for testing and, due to the holiday, the search parties had been suspended. Fitzgerald assured her that he had additional men coming in from Coleraine and other Garda stations, and that his men and the Kilargh volunteers would return to the search after All Soul's Day. He'd even pulled a few favors to have helicopter surveillance of the area.

"But we're a small village, Mrs. Dennistoun. We simply don't have the resources to keep at this ourselves."

She'd said something rude to him, she couldn't remember what, and had stormed from the station. She passed a trio of costumed children as she hurried down the street and didn't understand why that made her cry.

In her room at the Inn, she drank a bottle of wine and flipped through television channels. With her medication, she knew she shouldn't drink as much as she'd been doing, but tonight she didn't care. Every now and then, the doorbell rang below, and she heard muffled demands for candy from the town's children.

She found a television documentary on the history of the holiday, the kind of program Morgan would have stopped on to criticize for inaccuracies while secretly enjoying it.

"Samhain was a time when barriers fell," the narrator said in a thick Irish accent as shadowy dancers circled a bonfire. "It was when the veil between worlds was thinnest. It's no wonder, then, that Halloween rolls straight into All Saint's Day. If one wants to commune with things not quite human, there's no better time of year."

The wine had hit her system and the narrator's voice lulled her to sleep.

She dreamed of Morgan.

Her wife wore the same sweater and jeans she'd been wearing the day they'd first met on campus, only the clothes were now smeared with dirt and small twigs. Crumbled leaves were tangled in her hair and her skin had gone pale. She was in that church, torches burning peat all around her, and when Siân took a step forward, Morgan raised a hand.

Stop.

She trembled and her eyes glistened in the torchlight. Before Siân could say her wife's name, Morgan's hands went to her own mouth, covering it palm over palm as she shook her head.

Silence.

From behind her, bells jangled.

Siân sat up in bed, sleep still clinging to her and the bells echoing in her ears. A girl screamed on the television as some faceless slasher chased her across a porch covered in Jack-O-Lanterns. Siân turned the TV off.

Her phone said it was barely after two in the morning, but she didn't think she could immediately return to sleep. Light caught her eye from the window, and she leaned forward to see what it was.

A bonfire burned in a field not far from the Inn. A Halloween party still going strong. Costumed dancers circled the flames while others kissed and drank.

Someone sat just outside of the fire's light. Throne-like in shape, the strange chair they occupied seemed to be made from a thousand vines and branches twisted around themselves.

The figure leaned into the light. They wore a robe like a monk's cassock, a patchwork of red and purple and green cloth. Bells dangled from the elbows and knees and from rings on long, white fingers. She imagined she could almost hear them from across the field and through the closed window.

The mask this reveler wore resembled the skull of some large animal—a horse?—that stretched out from beneath a padded hood. Tassels fell from the hood, each ending in another bell, and they swung as it turned the dull white of its boned face toward her window.

She closed the curtains and turned the television back on.

At Kilargh's tiny cathedral the next morning, she stood in the back and listened as the priest said Mass.

"Last night may have been fun and games for most of you." A small chuckle from the assembly. "But this is the time of year we gather to not only remember those who have passed on, but to reach out to them. To offer them the love we still have in our hearts. Just because they are no longer with us does not mean they can't hear us. And by contemplating our love for them, we take a step toward our own salvation."

She left when the priest began speaking of the search efforts.

Fitzgerald leaned against the outside wall of the church, a long black coat buttoned to his neck, and puffed on a cigarette. She nodded to him and he held the cigarette out for her.

Smiling, she revealed her own pack.

"Not in a spiritual mood?" she asked.

"Might be I'm in too much of one," he said.

Across the street, an old woman balanced on a step ladder and ripped wet chunks of toilet paper from a massive tree.

"Don't know why she bothers," Fitzgerald said. "I'd just let the rain wash it all away. It'd break apart into nothing in a few days."

Siân almost said something about how sometimes you need to be active. How doing something, even when you know it's the wrong thing, is what keeps you from going insane. Instead she puffed away on her cigarette and pressed a pale piece of hard candy into the soil with her foot.

"Morgan used to paint. Acrylics, mostly. I hated that smell."

Fitzgerald turned to her, one eyebrow raised.

"I started dabbling in painting, too. Just for a few months. I thought it'd be fun, you know? Having a hobby that we shared."

"Was it?"

"She stopped painting about three weeks after I started. It was her thing and I had stolen it, I guess. I quit not long after that myself." She sucked a sharp breath and her voice broke. "See? That's what I do, Inspector. I quit things and... I don't know. I just... Morgan's the only thing I've ever been certain about in my life."

He nodded as though he could possibly understand.

"She has this... It's a curiosity, I guess. Seen half the world and tried every hobby or sport that ever interested her. She's like a moth in constant need of a flame. I always wished I could be like that." She sniffed. "But I can't just keep following her around, can I? It's not good for her."

"If you don't mind me saying, Mrs. Dennistoun, I don't think it's good for *you*."

She laughed, tears stinging her eyes, and dropped her cigarette to the dirt. "You're probably right," she said and ground the smoking butt down with her heel. "See you after the holiday, Inspector."

Climbing into the rental car, she went for an aimless drive. This had been her calming ritual since she'd first gotten her driver's license, sitting in her tiny metal box with the world moving by outside her window, no direction and no destination. In a way, it mimicked her life.

She called Aidan and was glad she'd gotten his voicemail.

"Hey, dick. It's me. If I catch a flight out Friday morning, can you pick me up from the airport? Just you, not Theresa and the kids. See you soon."

Admitting defeat had always been easy for her. Hell, Morgan might have said it was Siân's default mode. But this time was hard, and she knew she would break down when Aidan asked her about it. She'd rather get that out of the way without anyone else around.

After another half an hour of driving, she found herself on the road to the old church. She stopped across from where she thought the foot path started and wondered again why Morgan had spent so many days at such an uninteresting place.

Siân killed the engine, scribbled a note for the windshield saying where she'd gone in case she, too, got lost, and crossed the road into the woods. It took several minutes to find one of the stones marking the path. Though the day was gray and damp, the lack of rain made the trail much easier to follow. As she climbed the hill, she thought she smelled burning peat, but the odor vanished as quickly as it came.

As the clearing came into view, she caught sight of someone in the graveyard, waving their hands as though they tried to warn her away.

She stepped closer and a large raven took to the sky from where it sat on a tombstone. A trick of the light. She almost laughed.

Her nerves were raw, and she took a breath before continuing on across the clearing. Every noise she made, every twig that snapped or leaf that crunched beneath her feet, made her feel anxious and nervous, as though she trespassed, or tried to sneak up on someone and failed.

When she neared the church, the unmistakable sound of bells jangled from inside.

She stopped, the noise making her skin go cold. She thought of the bell Broderick had found and the sound she'd convinced herself she had not heard. Had someone been hiding in the dark when she was last here? She *had* felt watched.

Could that person know where Morgan was?

She rushed into the church. The interior was even darker than it had been the day before and she fumbled with her phone. The light came to life and she expected to see someone crouched in the darkness.

The place was empty.

Stepping farther inside, she again examined the place, certain she'd missed something, some hiding place a person could wedge themselves into, or even a small sculpture or engraving that might have intrigued her wife so much. She passed the same spots a dozen times, ran her hands over same moss-slick stones a dozen more, but there was nothing. No place to hide, and no indication of why Morgan had spent three days here.

The emptiness Siân felt pressed down on her. She gave up her search and sat on the fallen timber, tears threatening to overwhelm her.

The wood was soft and damp against her pants and tiny things scurried away from her to burrow deeper into the timber. She could imagine Morgan sitting in this exact spot, scanning the shadowed interior as she decided to leave Siân. Was there something here that had helped her decide? Something that added enough urgency to her decision to prevent waiting until the trip was over? If so, Siân couldn't see it now. She could only see the dead leaves and filthy water streaks, the spider webs and bat droppings, the cold moss and colder stone. She didn't know how long this church had sat abandoned, but she felt centuries of emptiness pressing in around her.

"Morgan," she said, her voice sounding hollow as it echoed from the stones.

She turned off the light to conserve her phone's battery and sat in the dark. Some part of her was certain this had been her fault. She knew that was ridiculous but couldn't shake the feeling. If she had only stayed in grad school, or kept the corporate job at a call center that she had hated so much but had paid their bills, or even if she had told Morgan she was right, that Siân did follow her like a puppy and she was sorry for it but was there anything really wrong with that? They loved one another, didn't they?

What was it that Morgan had been saving to tell her when she returned that evening? She'd said she wanted them to talk more about things and now Siân feared they never would. The questions would never end. Those wounds would remain open, festering until the day she died.

"I'll do better," she muttered. "I promise I will. I'll find my own life and leave you be when you need it. Just come back. Please."

The soft rustling of fabric made her spin and she almost fell from the rotten timber.

Was someone here with her?

She held her breath and didn't move. Phone clutched in one hand, she couldn't even bring herself to thumb the screen to life.

In the dark, the only light the dull silhouette of the entrance, she felt as though she were suddenly surrounded by people. The air heavy with the presence of a crowd, she could almost hear them breathing, could almost feel them brush against her as they shuffled back and forth. She told herself it was her medication but that didn't alleviate the unease. When she could no longer stand the feeling, she stood and darted for the door.

Outside the church and catching her breath, she turned her flashlight app back on. Shining it into the building, she was met with the sight that she expected.

Nothing.

Sliding the phone into her pocket, she leaned against the slick exterior of the church and closed her eyes.

Coming here again had been a mistake. Maybe Morgan had just slipped away to a nearby town to clear her head. She needed to wander, to explore, needed time alone more than Siân ever did. Siân hated time alone, hated the quiet and the excruciating memories her mind chose to dwell on when there were no distractions. When they'd first met, Siân was always dragging Morgan to a party or to hear a friend's band play, always planning last minute road-trips to romantic locales, always in search of a distraction. She had been interesting, once upon a time, before the pills and the tears. She'd been the kind of woman someone could fall in love with.

She'd said to Fitzgerald that Morgan was a moth in constant search of a flame. Yet Siân's own fire had been snuffed out somewhere along the way, whether by depression or medication or simply the tedious march into middle age, it didn't matter. Morgan needed something primal and fierce in her life while Siân had grown old and boring and only needed her pills, Morgan her pill of choice.

She should go back to the Inn, pack her bags, and book a flight home. This time tomorrow, she could be at her brother's house. Theresa would make a giant pot of coffee and the kids would climb all over her asking about Ireland. She and Aidan could hit that bar down the street. A few whiskeys and her brother's dumb jokes always made her feel better.

Scrambling around atop this hill had the opposite effect. She felt if she didn't leave now this place would drive her mad.

When she opened her eyes, determined to walk back down the hill and leave this Godforsaken country forever, she saw a figure at the edge of the wood.

Like the raven, she at first assumed it was a trick of light and shadow. Yet, even though it was at least a hundred yards away, she was positive a person stood behind the trees and watched her.

She took a few steps forward, hands shaking from fear, and thought there was something odd about the shape.

"Hello?"

Quiet.

She took another step and it came more into view. She couldn't quite make out their features, but the height and build were familiar.

Another step and the figure leaned out from behind the tree. Twigs and leaves were tangled in the hair and clothing but, even this far away, Siân recognized her. Her breath hitched and tears crashed hot onto her cheeks.

"Morgan?"

The figure turned and stepped back into the woods.

"Wait!" Siân ran toward what she was now certain was her wife. "Please!"

Crashing into the brush, Siân fought through the forest, twigs scratching her face, limbs tearing at her clothes. She fell twice, drying mud smearing her shirt and crumbled leaves tangling in her hair, but none of that slowed her down.

"Please! Just talk to me!"

What had Morgan been doing out here for over a week? Had she been lost? Had someone hurt her? Why was she running? Siân couldn't think through any of her questions, could only hurry on.

Morgan kept a steady pace, the distance between them never changing. No matter how fast Siân ran, or how much a thick tangle of brambles slowed her, the distance between them remained the same. Siân chased her downhill and uphill, through a stream and back again. It reminded her of playing chase with Aidan's kids, of how, no matter how fast she moved, they were quick enough to evade her. To play games with her. To taunt her.

She ran until her muscles burned and her lungs ached and then, through sheer desperation, ran more.

Finally, her body gave up on her and she fell to her knees, skidding through wet leaves before toppling over onto her hands. Every breath she took scorched her lungs despite the cold October air.

"Morgan," she panted, tears slick on her cheeks. "Why... are you..."

Between fighting for breath and the sobs now wracking her, she couldn't finish the question.

Morgan watched her from several yards away, her face small and pale nestled in the brush. Siân thought she looked like a fruit ready to be plucked and, in any other circumstance, the image would have made her laugh. Here it made her shiver.

The face retreated, vanishing into the green.

"Morgan? Don't go!"

The forest was silent, now. No footsteps. No twigs snapping. No brush pushed aside.

Shadows grew long as Siân knelt there, tired and alone. She leaned against a tree and pulled her knees to her chest. It would be dark soon. She was cold and damp and felt on the verge of a breakdown. Worst of all, she was lost. She couldn't remember from which direction she came. The forest was thick, the canopy dense overhead, and she could find nothing with which to get her bearings.

Bells jingled to her right. She stared into the dark growth, searched for some movement in the deepening shadows, but could find nothing.

Then the bells jingled again, and heavy footsteps crashed through the brush.

Siân was on her feet, panic flooding through her, as she sprinted again through the forest. She chanced to look behind her once, hoping she would see Morgan, and almost screamed.

A figure in a patchwork robe chased after her, its face a horse's skull.

The bells sounded furiously from behind her. Unlike Morgan, her pursuer did not keep pace with her. It gained on her steadily.

Dusk quickly turned the woods into a mosaic of purples and blacks. Siân did not have long until night fell, and she lost what little light she had.

She burst, then, into a small clearing not much larger than the break room at the Garda station. Yet the trees surrounding it somehow formed a perfect circle. The grass was a deep green despite the autumn and smelled of wet decay.

The sound of her pursuer stopped. No bells. No footsteps. She scanned the trees but could find no sign of the figure amidst the shadows.

"Morgan, I'll do better," someone said in a sing-song voice. "I promise I will."

The voice managed to be both gravelly and high-pitched. It made her bones tingle.

"I just need to be with you," it continued.

She spun, angry that anyone had heard her in the church, hurt that they would mock her pain.

There was no one there.

She turned back to the clearing and now saw two concentric rings of toadstools peeking through the green. They were white and gray and, like the space itself, geometric perfections.

The faint jangling of bells sounded again, and she gasped. It took her a moment to realize the noise came from within the rings.

She took a step forward and thought she could almost hear laughter. Maybe even music. It was so faint she couldn't be sure. But there was something.

"I'll do better," the voice taunted again.

Was it Morgan? Had it been Morgan who chased her?

Had it even been Morgan that she'd seen at all? Malicious little shapeshifters, Officer Broderick had said. Remembering that made Siân shiver.

She thought of what else Broderick had said of this hill and how Halloween was a time when the veil between worlds had thinned. It was dusk, now, on All Saint's Day. If she remembered her folklore correctly, the veil would strengthen again once night fell.

She thought of her dream and of the Lord of Misrule returning from the lands of the sidhe to preside over his court with a face carved from a horse's skull.

A breeze picked up just then and whispered in the rustling leaves of the trees. "Turn back," the wind said.

The breeze had Morgan's voice. Siân could tell by the way the leaves danced it originated from within the circle of toadstools.

"Please, Siân," the wind said. "I shouldn't have come here. Leave. No escape."

Crying, Siân took a step away from the clearing.

"You promised," the breeze said.

She had promised, hadn't she? To herself, to Fitzgerald, to Aidan, to whatever had spied on her at the church. She had promised to stop following Morgan around, to have her own life. Her own happiness.

More than to anyone else, she had meant that promise for Morgan.

The bells jangled, rapid and furious, and the breeze faded away. The faint voice, Morgan's voice, died with it.

The bells, though, continued to sound, the air heavy and tense as though someone had been caught doing something they weren't supposed to.

She wanted the breeze to return. Wanted to hear her wife's voice one last time.

The only sound in the clearing was the bells.

"I'm sorry, Morgan." Tears in her eyes, Siân laughed. "You know how horrible I am at keeping promises."

Knowing that every criticism her wife had ever lobbed at her was true, she took a deep breath and stepped into the ring of toadstools.

Night fell and the bells ceased to jangle.

ABOUT THE AUTHOR

Originally from East Tennessee, Brad C. Hodson is a novelist and screenwriter living in Los Angeles. A former stand-up comic and founder of an award winning sketch group, he currently works as the Administrator for the Horror Writers Association. He's written for page, screen, stage, and games (both video and tabletop), and loves storytelling in all its forms. In addition to several film and television projects in development, he's currently writing an upcoming comic book series for *WebToon*.

For more information on the author, or where you can find his other work, please visit www.brad-hodson.com.

Made in the USA
Coppell, TX
27 January 2020

15042406R00134